THE MOTORCYCLE CAFE

Matthew Condon is a reporter for the *Sun-Herald* in Sydney, having previously worked for the Brisbane *Courier-Mail* and the *Gold Coast Bulletin*. Born in 1962, he studied at the University of Queensland and the Goethe Institute, Bremen. His first play was produced while he was still at university. *The Motorcycle Cafe* is Matthew Condon's first book. He has received a grant from the Literary Arts Board, and is currently working on a further collection of related stories and also a novel.

To Caroline,
You better like it!

THE MOTORCYCLE CAFE

MATTHEW CONDON

for
Matthew.

University of Queensland Press
ST LUCIA • LONDON • NEW YORK

First published 1988 by University of Queensland Press
Box 42, St Lucia, Queensland, Australia

Typeset by University of Queensland Press
Printed in Australia by The Book Printer, Melbourne

Distributed in the UK and Europe by University of Queensland Press
Dunhams Lane, Letchworth, Herts. SG6 1LF England

Distributed in the USA and Canada by University of Queensland Press
250 Commercial Street, Manchester, NH 03101 USA

Creative writing program assisted by
the Literary Arts Board of the Australia
Council, the Federal Government's arts
funding and advisory body

Cataloguing in Publication Data

National Library of Australia

Condon, Matthew, 1962–
   The motorcycle cafe.
   I. Title.
A823'.3

British Library (data available)

Library of Congress

Condon, Matthew, 1962–
   The motorcycle Cafe / Matthew Condon.
      p.   cm.
   I. Title.

PR9619.3.C567M68   1988   87–34283
823–dc19

ISBN 0 7022 2132 5

for my mother and father,
with love and thanks

Contents

Acknowledgments   *ix*

Close to the Road   *1*
Darkroom   *12*
Cloud   *26*
The Motorcycle Cafe   *40*
The White Aeroplane   *56*
Weddings: The Guest   *67*
Mud and Ivory Elephants   *75*
Whalebone   *84*
Museum: from George's Notebook   *89*
Thieves   *100*
Envelopes   *111*
The China Doves   *121*
Weddings: The Best Man   *124*
Bias   *134*
Blue Overalls   *146*

Acknowledgments

"The Motorcycle Cafe" and "Thieves" have appeared in slightly different forms in *Australian Short Stories*, and "The White Aeroplane" in *Latitudes: New Writing from the North*, eds Susan Johnson and Mary Roberts (UQP, 1986). Portions of "Close to the Road" have appeared in *Chimera Literary Magazine* (Brisbane, 1983).

Sincere gratitude to Georgia "Jackie" Savage for her wisdom.

Close to the Road

George, my grandfather, rode a motorcycle he called Satan. He painted the name on both sides of the black fuel tank, and on one side, a devil's head. The skin of the devil fiery orange. The horns red. The devil had a thin moustache, and his friends at the motorcycle club said if you scraped off the thin lines of black paint, the devil would look like George.

He kept his powerful machine perfectly clean and draped a white sheet over it at night. My grandmother, Frieda, was scared of the motorcycle, its side mirrors and pedals poking out under the sheet. Especially when she put out the rubbish at the bottom of the back stairs and it was there, under the house, in the dark.

For years she asked him to call it another name and paint over the devil's face, but he refused. When George died, not long after he sold the motorcycle to a local dealer, she scratched out the name in a photograph of the machine with a ball-point pen. She pressed so hard the pen broke through the surface of the picture.

Frieda once asked him why he called it Satan and he said that's how he felt when he rode. As if he was on fire, or that something menacing was chasing him.

When he rode late at night through Brisbane streets his skin tingled, as if he had already fallen, and speed and bitumen had burnt through his leather jacket and trousers.

George never had a bad accident but every time he rode off, after an argument or just to get away, my grandmother imagined him falling on a sharp bend, slamming into a fence, clipping a gutter and tumbling, and was only relieved when she heard the growl of the motorcycle in the space under the house, and George's heavy boots up the back stairs.

She never asked him where he had gone. She just waited, countless times, for him to return from the dark.

*

I first started running when I was born, so my grand-father had said. In the giant glass tear of the hospital crib. My legs, as thin as pencils, pumped at the faces of nurses and relatives. From that day I was known as the runner.

After filing all day at work I would drive home through housing estates and into the blue gravel driveway of my parents' house. The gravel crunches under the wheels of my car. Tiny bushfires racing.

The house where I live is the white wooden dream of my mother. When she was a child, she had the shape of the house in mind. Its steep roof. The windows full of lace. Bull nosed steel awnings and the long verandah across the front. She helped design the house. She drew sketches of it on a small notepad, free from the local pharmacist, and gave the loose sheets to the architect. He drew larger, more precise plans, and left out my mother's inky shrubs, flocks of birds, sunsets.

There are only a few houses in our area, spread apart at the base of a wooded hill. The land close to my mother's house is cleared of trees, but there are weeds. Taller than my father, with long green stalks that whistle in a breeze. They sway together, and are brushed by the fur of rabbits and wallabies that live in the hill scrub and come down to the houses in search of garden vegetables, or water.

I prepare for my afternoon run in my upstairs room, stretching tight muscles to music, and can see the hill through my window. The stretching takes a long time but makes the run easier on the hard roads. It takes more than strong legs to run the roads. When I've warmed up I go outside for more preparation. Driving my shoes into veins of clover that bruise dark green.

*

George used to race at a track outside Brisbane. A dirt track on private property not far from a creek belt. It was an odd-shaped circular rut that buckled around granite outcrops and gums, a foot deep into the soil.

His motorcycle club put up an old army tent in the middle of the circuit every weekend. A small clicking generator pumped electricity into a race caller's microphone. They had no problems with the cows. They were pushed to the edges and corners of the paddock in leather clusters, or hard against barbed wire fences, afraid of the noise.

After the races the men drank beer into the night. The riders slept in the back of trucks, or on the grass, and in the morning the cows would wake them, tearing grass from the earth inside the track. Grazing amongst the motorcycles.

The club used the track for years until the farmer sold his motorcycle and his property. They say the track is still there, the ruts grown over with a net of runners. In heavy rain it still fills with water. And the cows make a quick leap to its lush centre.

*

My cat, Cheek-Pook, sits on a white cane chair on the verandah on a soft cloth pillow covered in faded pears and avocados. The cat stares into the valley, beyond the dead tree near the house, its branches stiff like the up-turned feet of a bird. I sit on a chair next to the cat and tie my laces. I hear the popping of the cat's claws as they burst into an avocado.

I run down the first hill. The road is new. Smooth and grey through vacant lots and weeds. The early part of the run is easy. Gentle, like floating on a river in a rubber dinghy. Pushed by a mild breeze.

People work in their yards in the late afternoon when I run. Crush grass with their bare feet, still white and tender from office shoes. The history of wooden implements through their skin as they take a rake, or a pick, from toolsheds. I see one couple every afternoon, labouring with rocks.

"Hello," they say into stone, my scissoring legs in the corner of their eyes.

Their house is the same shape as the letterbox. Their yard like the surface of the moon. Mounds of topsoil. Ranges of it down the side of the house. No plants, only dirt and rocks.

They have been working for months on a rock

garden, pushing boulders into circles. They make different patterns with the rocks, continually changing the art that is their front yard. White-painted river stones border the driveway.

The doberman in the next yard sits by the wire fence and watches the couple. It ignores me as I run past and looks at the straining figures, rolling rocks. It twitches its muzzle or wiggles the bulb of its tail. It is entranced by the moving landscape and raises its nose to savour the smell of human sweat.

*

The shop used to be a hairdressing salon before George and his friend moved in. Clumps of dead hair, swept together or pulled from brushes, were left in corners and between floorboards. The shop even smelled of singed hair. George spent an hour scraping off the long burgundy locks of a woman painted on the shop window. They came off in solid pieces under the razor blade, the cream face thinner, powdery.

George made motorcycle jackets, gloves and boots and his friend Dave started a repair workshop out the back. It was George's idea to open the shop and it wasn't long before a lot of Brisbane riders were wearing his products. He tailored them for each rider. Traced around their outstretched hands for the gloves. Put their names on the paper hand patterns and kept them in a box, for the future.

His club held their meetings in the shop. Pictures of riders hung from the walls and trophies stood on a shelf behind the counter. When the suburb went quiet, and the business died, George still went around to the shop.

It was vacant for years and inside he could still smell the leather.

He would sit in there and think, or look out the front window through the shape of the woman's head, still visible but scratched and cleaner than the rest of the glass, and watch the traffic.

*

When I get to the first corner I run in an arc across the road. I have seen rabbits do the same at night. They burst out of weeds that grow to the concrete guttering and swing across the warm bitumen. They appear most-ly in winter, just as the sun sets, and the steepness of the hills makes them run in loops. Briefly warmed by headlights and back into the damp lots.

I work up another hill and wonder what gravel has been skittered by their feet. Where their tracks are, crooked with the fear of car wheels and light and death, on the road. They seem to wait for the cars before they perform their awkward dance.

The first few hills are the easiest to get over. I take shorter steps, keep my head down and focus on the road. Feel the grain of muscles and the pores open. The air is flecked with small cyclones of bugs. A cockatoo, sitting in a cage under the awning of a house, cries out at about the same time every day. It must hear me plod-ding, or accidentally kicking stones. It starts the dogs barking.

I carry a quartz rock in my hand because of the dogs. At dusk it is hard to see them race out from the sides of houses or leap off verandahs. I only hear them when they are on the road and their nails click on the hard sur-face. Cream teeth like rows of broken tea cup handles.

6

Small dogs as worn as leather bags. Others reclining on front lawns, chewing huge bones, knuckles.

I have reached the halfway point of the run at the house with a yard full of car bodies. A man pounds metal in the garage. The cars are right around the house. A green sedan down the side. A ute near the clothesline. An old Morris beside the letterbox. His front gate is a small red car door.

I have only ever seen the man's legs, poking out from under a bonnet in the garage. He strips parts from the car bodies and tries to build one workable vehicle. There is a bicycle near the front door.

As I run past his spotted dog jumps through the glassless windscreen of a wreck. On other days it might appear from an open boot, or under a dashboard. The dog growls and tries to frighten me, but I am ready for it. It waits until the last minute, and I see its tail, like a windscreen wiper, or its ear, inside the wreck.

Opposite the house is a children's park but I have never seen children there. The swings are made of un-painted iron pipes and wood. Blood rust on small hands. And in the centre of the park is a large fibreglass egg that spins.

The children are probably eating now, wolfing their food so they can creep into the park. Make secret bird calls over fences, and sit and giggle in the shadowy egg.

*

My mother said George had nearly as many cars and trucks in his life as the copies of Popular Mechanics magazines he stacked around the house. She remembered the magazines and always the most recent issues next to his chair in the loungeroom. He put empty

7

coffee mugs and plates of biscuits on them until the pile rose above the armrest of the chair and began to lean. Then he put them in the spare room, and later in boxes downstairs. He never threw a single copy away.

Once he took my mother in Satan's sidecar to a farm house near Samford. She had her own special helmet with her name in fine loops on its sides and blue stars painted on the crown. She loved riding so close to the road in the sidecar, her red sandals somewhere in the front of the black capsule. Looking up at faces and hats in car windows. Other children looking down at her, their palms pressed against glass. They rode beneath canopies of gums on the dirt roads beyond the city and into the valley of neat crops and dams.

At the farm my mother chased chickens and stroked rabbits, poking her fingers into their wire cages. George looked over the spoke-wheeled Ford in the barn. The farmer stood near the barn door as George walked around the truck, kicked the tyres, sat in the cabin and looked at a wall of tools through the windscreen.

He bought the truck and fixed it up. He painted it with a spraygun under the house and the fumes came up through the floorboards. They could smell the paint in their sleep for days after. He eventually sold the truck and bought another one.

George never owned a car, my mother said, he just liked to keep them for a while and get them into shape again. To make them new again, although they weren't.

He had just finished repairing a ute before he died. Fitted new tyres and a shiny black radiator. Changed its oil. His friend came and took it away when my grandmother went to Sydney to recover from George's death. The man drove the truck to his empty garage by the bay, his arm out the window, the motor gently ticking. An empty paint tin and George's tools in the back.

*

When I run for home the mountains are pale pink. The houses in the estate I travel through are all the same. It's as if builders had squatted on the dirt pads of each lot and swivelled in their centres a common plan. The bedroom of one house facing the street. The same bedroom in the house next door looking out over a clothes hoist.

But the yards are different. One house has a driveway of bark pieces. The next, a splay of tiny pebbles embedded in concrete. A clipped hedge across one yard, meeting a neighbour's row of rose bushes. Down the sides of the houses, however, I see the rows of singlets or underwear on clotheslines. Plastic pegs like rows of silent birds. Incinerators and compost heaps in the corners.

I can smell the meals as I reach the top of the hill. That savoury smell that lingers in the streets at dusk and never leaves some houses, right through curtains, bed quilts, lampshades.

I approach the final stretch home and run quickly down the hill. The weeds are tall on either side of the road. At the bottom there is always a cold band of air. Somewhere, beneath the bitumen, a buried creek bed. An invisible whale of air that plays with the weeds, and turns sweat ice cold.

I sprint through the air patch, chilling in the absence of streetlights. It is always there at the bottom of the hill. A danger, a fear I cannot grasp. I have to go through it, though, as there is no other way home.

*

George only had one serious accident at the track, although he fell off many times. He broke a bone in his right foot. He was leading a race when he slowed at a turn and was slammed into a soil bank by another rider. Satan fell on his foot.

He finished the race. Frieda cried as they walked the motorcycle to his truck.

"Played it too safe and they caught me," George said, checking the motorcycle for damage. He spent the rest of the afternoon in the truck, his bandaged foot poking out through the open car door.

He often boasted that he was not afraid to fall, but my grandmother showed me the list in his notebook. George carried it with him most times and scribbled poems and sketches in it.

But at the back there was a list of my grandfather's "close-calls". Descriptions and dates of accidents avoided in Brisbane suburbs. A neat list of street names, times of the day, details of drivers' faces and the colour and make of their cars. Walls and fences he could have been thrown into. Trucks and buses that could have cut short his life.

He may have exaggerated his brushes with death, my grandfather. Collected the incidents like a boy does stamps, or marbles. He didn't know then the cancer had caught him. When he did, he no longer wrote of any close-calls in his notebook.

*

It is dark now and I tread on a large stone. It unsettles my balance and my left knee buckles. A few steps later and I regain the rhythm. A stone can fell a runner. Break bone in a clean twist or tattoo a bruise on a thick-skinned heel.

I am wary of cars as I run over the final hill. It is a silent drop, as if the trees and weeds alter sound at that point in the road. I have run down it and not known of approaching cars until their final shift of gears. A delivery van shoots over the hill, the headlights illuminating my white socks, and I step to the other side of the road. As it rushes past I feel the warm, oily wave of air. Weed seeds swirl. A sedan follows closely behind and I wince as sweat runs into my eyes.

I swim in my parents' pool after a run. The cooling down time is too real and everything is sharp, clear, when I stop. Moth wings against streetlights. Warped tree bark at different angles. I float near the steps in the pool wearing only my running shorts. Even in the cold water there is an aura of heat around my body. Later, I sink down into the water with only my head exposed, and the shadows of the hills on the surface of the pool run up to my neck and taste of chlorine.

One day the run through the streets, the fields of rabbits, will not hurt. It will be a perfect combination of breaths, strides, dreams. As a runner I know I may only achieve that once.

Sharp yellow headlights swoop nearby. The pool gets colder and if I sit still, thousands of litres of water ebb to my heartbeat.

Darkroom

My grandmother always said she taught me how to drink tea. She drank hers black, in a mug with quickly painted roses on its surface. You could almost see the blur of hand and brush beneath the glaze. When I visited, she gave me her best cup and saucer.

We sat at a table in the small kitchen at the back of her fibro house. A white house with dark blue trimming on the gutters and window ledges. Years ago, I remembered, the ledges were painted green and it came off, powdery, on your forearms or hands.

Early in the century men had lifted the house onto stumps. Rusted railway tracks, pulled from the earth of forgotten country lines, held the house above the block of land. When the house was first placed on the stumps and steel my grandmother said it groaned and creaked in the night, and as she rested in bed, she thought the rumble of years of travel and passengers had been pressed into the tracks.

The laminex table in the kitchen was the same one I had sat at for hundreds of childhood meals. I counted the crude gold stars on its surface when I ate. Pretended it was the galaxy I saw on television in the afternoons. A block of the universe held up by four thin metal legs. Like all my family's discarded furniture, it found its way into my grandmother's house.

Every time she finished her tea she tilted the mug and drained it to the end. Tea leaves would freckle her lips. She rolled the mug in her hands and studied the wreckage of leaves. She fancied herself as a sort of fortune teller. She saw animals in the mug. Soggy elephants or dogs. Floating mice. She didn't know if they possessed any greater meaning, she just saw them.

During the second cup of tea she spoke of afternoons with friends in nursing homes, herself hugging grocery bags like papery relatives down the hill near her home, and methods of keeping her monstrous cat, Sixpence, cool in summer. And when the tea in the bottom of our cups turned lukewarm she talked about my grandfather, George. He watched me all the time in the kitchen. From the shelf against the wall, where her fish tank had been before her goldfish was found floating upside down and bound with reeds, a photograph of George.

The frame was silver-looking metal and shaped like cuttings of bamboo, dull and spotted with rust. George's hair resembled a small cloud in front of a pale blue studio backdrop. Hair prematurely white and whispy. He stared at the side of the frame, his face light grey. A shadow, like the heel of a boot, rested under his chin.

I imagined he was dying then, behind the sliver of glass. Dying when he went to the studio in Queen Street and sat on the stool in front of the blue sheet that hung from a wooden bar near the ceiling. Looking into the tangle of wires and lights and trying to smile for my grandmother, years after his death.

My grandmother cleaned the table after tea, her slippers scuffing on the linoleum floor. They were tattered slippers with fluffy red material on the top, like the windblown poinsettia flowers on her front lawn. She told stories of George as she washed the cups. The best looking man in Brisbane, she said. His signwriting and love of photography. She wiped crooked lines of ants from around her cat's milk saucer. She hated ants, and the way they stood side by side at the fringe of the souring milk.

I went to the drawer I had been going to since I was a boy. It was at the end of the kitchen cabinet, painted pink inside with a rectangular compartment at the back. The drawer was my own museum. A wooden corridor that held the artefacts of my grandfather. A hammer with a smooth handle and rounded head. Thick blue pencils. Matches and toothpicks. A large clear marble covered in scratches. It was, I imagined as a child, the eye of an old man.

And there was the key with the brass nameplate. I took the key, walked past my grandmother who rinsed the tea pot in the sink, the leaves swirling in running water, and went down the back steps to the darkroom.

*

"Shut the door Jack or you'll ruin the film," George said.

A twig of yellow light from the open door disappeared and they waded in red from the single bulb. White shapes wobbled for a moment before their eyes, then objects emerged in the darkroom. Rows of jars and bottles. The bulky picture printer. The porcelain sink.

"You think they'll come out all right?" Jack said. He tended to whisper in the darkroom. It was quiet apart from the occasional breath of a passing car. A dog's bark.

14

"They should do, although the last lot weren't too bloody good," George said. "I think that bodgie Chinaman in the Valley sold me the wrong stuff."

George bathed a wide strip of film in chemicals in the sink. The liquid swayed, sometimes rising above the sink lip and splashing on the floor. Their leather jackets and boots creaked in the dimness. Folds and zips blood red.

"I have another film I want to do while I'm here," George said. "You don't mind, do you mate?"

Jack was trapped in the darkroom. If he walked out the light would burn and destroy everything. He sat on the stool and rubbed his left knee. Caked mud from the track dropped to the floor. He had fallen at the cycle races.

"Here's a good shot of Jim and Snake on the line," George said. "A bloody beauty."

They looked through the negatives in front of the red bulb. Toy cycles in scarlet frames. Men with piercing white eyes. The officials' tent at the track like a felt hat in the dust. Heat and speed.

"There's Micko on one wheel. He'll be dead soon if he keeps that up. Silly bastard."

Jack sniffed. The same dust in George's negatives was in the creases and pockets of Jack's coat. Every weekend at the races it settled over them. In the negatives, statues.

"I'll print them tomorrow and give them to the boys," George said.

He took a film cartridge from his pocket and developed it in the chemicals still swaying from the pace of the riders. He told Jack he found the film in an old suitcase and wanted to see who had been trapped inside the roll for so long. Jack sat on the stool and thought of cool beer at the club.

George looked through the dark shapes on the surface

of the chemicals and saw the woman appear. Several pictures of the woman, her teeth and eyes pale pink. George held her up to the red bulb.

He hung the film on a rack at the back of the darkroom. He switched off the light, opened the door and they stumbled into pink and grey to their motorcycles parked on the front lawn.

Still adjusting to the light, George started his cycle, put on his goggles and had to duck beneath the poinsettia tree as he rode out into the street. The flowers, bright red, vicious, whipped at the goggle glass and for a moment he remembered the evil clown that had scared him when he was a child, at a carnival.

*

I felt uneasy every time I unlocked the wooden door to the darkroom because I always expected my grandfather to be waiting in there for me. An old man, bent on the stool, his wrinkled hand in the cool chemicals of the sink.

The darkroom was a small wooden cubicle in the corner under the house. I could hear my grandmother moving upstairs. Into the dining room to polish the black piano, or dusting odd-sized photograph frames in my mother's old bedroom.

When I was younger I sat in my grandfather's old Buick. It was anchored to the concrete under the house by its four flat tyres. For years he had promised to replace them and fix up the car, but the wheels rested on the rubber until the rims cut through to the cold concrete. I used to stare through the windscreen like a fish in a bowl and watch the darkroom door. I sat on crazed leather seats that crackled when you moved and played with cream knobs on the dash. The bonnet of the massive car lunged forward.

It was scary for a child, inside the darkroom. A straw hat rested upside down on the floor. A rake, shovel and pick leaned into one corner. The sink was choked with rubbish. A drowned man's mouth, so I thought. It was a place separate from the rest of the world.

Some of the fear disappeared as I grew older. Once inside I felt I knew the room. What was on the shelves, in the small drawer of darkness under the bench. I even knew the height of the hook screwed to the back of the door. I moved from sink to shelves as I imagined George would have. I moved around in the dark like those people pushing themselves through developing strips of film in the sink.

Old film, curled and split, hung from a wire rack at the back. There were cuts of film in the corners of the room. Whiskers of grass. Newspapers. I took a few strips of film, turned on the light and fully closed the door.

The bulb was clear, not red as I always expected. The empty cardboard shells of lightbulb packages were on the floor. The arcing filament burned as I held the film to it. I only glanced at the images because the light was too bright. Painful, through the legs of trousers, helmets, teeth. There were girls, too. Smooth arms and shoulders. Rounded muscles. A striped bathing costume. A petrol pump and a man wearing goggles. Two babies. Dogs.

I turned off the light and sat in the dark. A knife-cut of light appeared across my shoe. I could not remember ever seeing that piece of light. I had been sitting on the stool in the dark for years. I was familiar with the dozens of fine cracks in the darkroom's floor and walls that made it float. The glow of compressed light lifted it

17

from its base of short concrete stumps until I thought, after some time, that if I stood up from the stool and opened the darkroom door I would see clusters of red iron roofs and the crowns of poinciana trees, heavy with spindly black pods, below.

The new light was singing with sharpness. I turned the light on again and moved the stool over to the bench, then climbed towards the crack in the ceiling.

A fibro panel had shifted. I could hear my grandmother upstairs, walking through the house. Years of movement, shifting furniture and maybe the vibration of bass from the black piano had unsettled the panel. It had taken decades. Even the body weight of my grandfather would have travelled through wooden floorboards and nails, to the darkroom ceiling.

I pushed back the panel and pieces of plaster fell on my hair, forearms and bench. It was a small opening, and I reached into the space between the darkroom ceiling and the floor of the house. It was a cool passage of air. Lit by the glow from backyard grass. Just beneath my grandmother's bedroom, in that fleshy gap of dust and air, I found the hand-made satchel.

I pulled it through the opening and held it, my skin as cool as its leather. Sitting on the stool, under the light of the Woolworths bulb, I untied the leather strap and met the true George for the first time.

*

"George, you've got another parcel from Elaine," Jack said on the telephone. "Want to come and pick it up?"

"Thanks mate, I'll be over soon," he said.

He had to squint to see into the kitchen. Sunlight through the louvres struck the linoleum. Fused rose patterns, petals. Frieda was standing at the sink, in the glare. He put the heavy black mouthpiece on the hook. The brown cord, frayed and speckled with stars, curled against the wall like a noose.

George went back to the kitchen table and rolled a cigarette. He thought of the hedges in front of the boarding house where he once lived. Chimney pots, wires, fog. The lines of the street gutter, the hedge, the house drains, and the open sky.

"Another cup of tea?" Frieda asked.

"That'd be nice, ta," he said.

"Have you finished those jackets yet?" she said, putting the kettle on the stove. The pop of gas. A blue hiss.

"I ran out of leather on the last one. Didn't have enough for the arms."

He looked into his half-full tobacco pouch. Sprinkled some grains on his palm. She brought him a mug of black tea and as he sipped the steam touched the oil on his face.

"Where's Anne?" he asked. He had not seen his daughter all day.

"She's playing mother with the girl next door. I gave her a few pegs and some old tea towels. She wants to know when her bike will be fixed."

"Will you get off my back about the bloody bike?" he said. "I have got work to do you know. I'm the one who has to put food on the table."

He grabbed his leather jacket and cap from a hook near the back landing and walked out. She sat alone at the table and looked into his mug. The steam had gone and the tea leaves had drifted into a pile at the bottom.

The roar of George's motorcycle shook the fibro house. Squeezed fat cigar notes from the piano in the dining room. He rode out into the street and before the cloud of exhaust had lowered and dissolved from the yard, Frieda had started crying.

Jack sat in his front room and listened to a radio. As George's motorcycle clattered up the street the race caller's voice began breaking up until he could not hear it. Moisture from a beer bottle dripped onto the horses' names in race five at Eagle Farm, on the yellow form guide. George came up the back stairs.

"You got the parcel?"

Jack reached down beside his chair and handed him the brown package. It was bound with string. Stamps and fine loopy handwriting.

"When you going to tell Frieda, George?" Jack said. "I'm getting tired of this. Better tell her soon or something's going to go wrong."

"Mind your own bloody business," George said.

He went back down the stairs and rode away. Jack could hear the caller again. The field had lined up at the gates. The bugle sounded. The barrier broke.

George went to the old motorcycle shop, the parcel against his chest inside the leather jacket. The breeze cool. String warming.

He still had a key to the back door, although he had moved out of the shop years before. A real estate agent had planned to set up in the shop some time later with cabinets, maps and boxes of pins, but it never eventuated. Someone had boarded up the front door.

In the afternoons the sun pushed through dusty glass facing the street. Particles swam through yellow. George sat on an old chair and put his feet up on a ledge. From the outside, passing motorists could have caught a glimpse of him there, an image almost part of the filthy

20

glass. A blue letter and roll of film rested on his lap.

He knew what was inside the black film cartridge. The woman and her family. The stony beach. Flat crowds. Trees of a different hemisphere. Pictures the photographer would never see, or know were in focus. Or whether they were taken in too much or not enough light.

George rode for hours through unfamiliar suburbs. He never asked for directions when he lost his way, but went back over his tracks, looked into dim streets at intersections, rested in parks and followed heavy traffic. If he got caught in dead-ends, he would look to the low cloud cover for signs of headlight flow.

Even as the wind tore past his ears on the way home, he could still hear the crack of the white chair in the empty motorcycle shop and see the flecks of paint that rose and fell like shot geese.

*

They were old photographs, printed on the blue paper my grandfather always used. The woman was not beautiful, but pleasant. Her hair was cut in the style of the day. Her lips were moist, and if I could have looked behind the surface of the print, they would have been red.

I could hear the chug of a mower in a backyard not far away. It was a gritty, sharp sound. I thought of fresh grass and green-stained feet and bees.

The letters were tied together with string, addressed to a house in a nearby suburb. George must have lived there when he first came to Brisbane. In one of those houses that now huddle between office blocks, right in the city, their backyards squares of grass, looked into from building windows. Not just over fences, like in the early days. I wasn't sure.

The letters were sentimental and made me laugh. Once, they may have been serious, but it was hard to imagine with that gap of time, that space of cool air, that separated now and then.

I was reading another letter and holding photographs of the woman when the floorboards creaked above the darkroom. I felt shadows shift. Wood tighten. I flicked off the light and sat in the darkness.

*

A dog's bark corkscrewed around the streetlights. They had frilly tin covers above the bulbs, their shadows the wobbly bases of full skirts on the bitumen. A stream of cockroaches flowed from a streetlight near the fibro house to an open drain. Cracked wings littered the base of the lamp pole.

George crept down the back stairs and into the darkroom. He filled the sink with chemicals, took the film from his robe pocket and developed the brown strip. Later he held the film to the red light. Liquid ran across his veined hands and down his forearms. The woman's hair was parted on the wrong side. It was not as he remembered. He turned the film around.

Some of the frames had not come out. There were dark squares between a face, or a building. The pictures were not in any sequence so he could only guess what the light had burned away.

He leaned against the bench for a while and the moist film dropped to the floor. Dust and pieces of grass clung to its surface, scratching the images. Tattoos that would

emerge later on the prints. He went back to the warmth
of his bed.

*

Air flowed under the darkroom, around concrete
stumps, weeds, and up through cracks in the floorboards. A piece of straw shivered. The photographs
warmed in my hand. Blood in my thumb heating a
strange woman's breast.

I had seen her before, in some of the sketches my
grandmother had framed on her dresser. She looked
younger in ink lines. On lemon paper, wearing hats
shaped like bells, pearls, scarves. Perhaps the sketches
were really of my grandmother, drawn so long ago that
even the sketches themselves became similar,
anonymous, as the faces of people do with age.

My grandmother thought it was herself in the frames
on the dresser. She often told me of that hat, which was
really green and not yellow as the picture depicted, and
the string of pearls she had saved for after years of
cleaning and ironing in the house of Brisbane's
wealthiest woman, whose drawers were stuffed with
gold brooches and rings and lined, not with paper, but
silk scarves. They could have been any woman's pearls
in the drawing, stretched around a neck of two black
lines.

I wondered if my grandfather was too secretive. He
kept quiet about things and carried them, like parcels
under his arms, into death.

*

23

George wanted to destroy the white aeroplane many times. The toy plane stood in the corner under the house with a blanket draped over it. Two motionless propellors and the tail jutted up under the blanket which did not touch the ground, but wavered just above the concrete. In an afternoon breeze the plants on a shelf near the toy shook, as did the blanket edges, and the aeroplane appeared to make an attempt at flight.

He spent hundreds of hours making the aeroplane, before and after the birth of his daughter. They had flown together through summer air, the smell of soil during a sudden downpour, and pockets of gas that leaked from the pipe under the house.

He had taken a hammer to it once. Struck the wing with such force it left a bruise the shape of the hammer's head and cracked layers of paint. But he could not destroy it. It had become a part of his space there, on the square of concrete, even though Anne could no longer fit in the tiny cockpit.

After he printed the photographs, put them in the leather satchel, poked it through the hole in the darkroom ceiling and replaced the panel, he locked the wooden door and sat in his cane chair next to the workbench. He looked at the dark aeroplane shape in the corner.

*

It must have been distance that made his other life so real. My grandfather didn't really tell lies, he just created another person in himself. Started to believe his own dream. He couldn't let people go out of his life. Collected them like some people do match boxes, or old drink coasters. Never had the courage to say goodbye.

I heard the kettle sing upstairs and looked up for a moment. The open letters were scattered around my feet. Pages of them rocking on old folds. I smiled because I was a conspirator with him. We shared a secret. He was dead, but I could understand the pain the letters must have caused. I could almost feel his red shape moving around in the darkroom. The texture of his overalls.

I heard a noise, close. Crunching gravel, or a scuff. I sat still when the darkroom door swung open and the painful light fell on me. A rush of air, and the letters staggered like drunken blue birds.

I squinted into the natural light and saw the outline of my grandmother. Wavy hair and her thin legs poking out from the square base of her dress.

My skin tingled in waves. First the face and ears then the arms and thighs, as if the light had touched me at different times. Even through jeans and a cotton shirt.

"What are you doing?" my grandmother said. "I've just made another pot of tea."

Cloud

The house where my grandfather died reminded me of eggs. For years I spent childhood vacations in the house by the bay. My sister and I would wake up early, the cry of birds tinkling from the shore, and our Great Aunt Nell would boil the eggs.

We would sit at the table in the cold rectangular kitchen and watch her, stooped over a saucepan, the steam billowing around her shoulders and head. I recall the whiskers on her chin, a burning white, as she dropped the eggs into china cups with ducks painted on their sides.

I hated boiled eggs but she stood over me until I ate them. I would dip bread into the runny yolk, and rock the head of the egg on the plate to take my mind off the smell. The smell is there now, in bone behind my nose and cheeks, planted there in my childhood.

The green house was full of shells. A large, pearly shell lamp stood on the television. Light would bounce off its rainbow surface, and I wondered what fish had nibbled at it when it once rested on the sea bed. The sideboard was filled with smaller shells. Some with spots like the skins of African animals. Others with spidery

26

limbs held to the back of the cabinet by fine webs. Open shells that held the bodies of insects. There were shells on the window ledge, facing the bay, and a giant clam shell that held back the kitchen door.

Aunt Nell's husband had been a diver. His large brass helmet sat on a shelf in a shed behind the house. I avoided the shed when I was young because I expected to find his head trapped in that chamber of brass and glass. He dived for pearl and collected shells. Over the years the shells in the house moved, when a cabinet was knocked or the curtains flicked inwards in a breeze. It was as if they were shifted by a tide and naturally scattered.

At times it appeared the beach was being drawn into my aunt's house. Sand lodged in the cracks of the red clay stairs leading up to the front door, in between floorboards and around nails. Shoes would grate on sand on the kitchen floor and at night, when I lay in the soft bed on the verandah, I could hear the lapping of waves and feel sand with my toes between the sheets.

My sister and I would go down to the shore and look for shells of our own. They were often dry, tangled in the hair of seaweed and just visible through the brown strands. One day I thought I found a sea horse but it was a stiff piece of weed, black and curved.

We would carry the shells, clinking in our hands, back to the house. But often we dumped them in long grass along the way because they could never match the beauty of the shells in our aunt's house.

It was an eerie place, with salty curtains and a strange coolness. When I think of that house now I see colourful shells, varnished, spotted and smooth, pink and spiky, curled like bunched fists or splayed and flat. And I smell freshly cracked eggs.

*

27

"Here's your coffee, George," Frieda said.

He was propped up in bed, looking out the bedroom window through the pink curtain. The road a dark salmon strip. Fleshy trees. A red bird swooped past, pale grey in the break of the curtain.

George rolled a cigarette, his hands hard and creased. They were speckled with paint, as they had been most of his life. His arms were thin, the skin sallow. They poked from his baggy flannelette pyjama shirt. The skin of his neck was strained and dry. For years tiny clouds of cigarette smoke had passed across it.

Tobacco fell on the white sheet across his waist. He flicked it onto the embroidered roses of the quilt.

"Did you bring those little biscuits?" he asked.

"The ones with jam in them?"

"Yes. The jam ones."

"I didn't think you liked that sweet jam," Frieda said.

"Yes. I want those ones."

He ate recklessly when he was ill. He was like a weird king, upright in that feather bed, eating out of time and place. Bacon and eggs in the early afternoon. Apple pie at dawn.

He turned on the radio at his bedside and she went back to the kitchen. She could hear muted notes through the white plastic grille of the radio speaker. Frieda took the eggs out of the saucepan, put them on the steel sink and they skidded together into running water.

"Do you still want these eggs, Doigy?" she said. She started using his nickname again since he had been ill. She fussed over him. Read him funny stories from the newspaper. Fluffed up his pillow before he slept.

"Ta," he said. "You know Jack is riding today, Frieda?"

She placed the eggs in small white cups and carried

them on a tray into the bedroom. A thin branch of blue smoke drifted to the ceiling. He had lit another cigarette.

"Why don't you put that out and eat these while they're still warm," she said.

He scooped off the heads of the eggs with a spoon.

"This one's got a blood spot, look," he said.

He ate them slowly, the radio music swaying gently with the curtains. A motorcycle clattered in a nearby street and he held still the spoon for a moment, then continued to eat the eggs.

The doctor came to see George every second day. He was short with grey hair, and wore a black suit. He carried a fat leather bag.

George didn't like the doctor and the sweet, scrubbed smell of his hands. The smell made him cringe, and he hated the instruments, cold and steely, in the bag.

The doctor called him "Cloud" because he smoked so much.

"You really should stop smoking," the doctor said. "Especially considering the condition you're in."

"What the hell have I got left, doc?" George said, snorting smoke through his nostrils, like motorcycle exhaust.

"You should be in hospital."

"This is my hospital."

"The man's impossible," the doctor said, and walked out of the bedroom.

Frieda spoke with the doctor at the bottom of the front stairs, under the limbs of the poinsettia tree. They whispered, even though George couldn't hear them, and glanced at his bedroom window.

"Some sea air might do him the world of good," the doctor said. "Could you take him to the sea for a while?"

"His sister has a house at Sandgate," Frieda said.

"Try and talk him into it, will you?"

The doctor plodded across the road to see Mrs Olsen. The street was dying, and he had a lot of calls to make.

It rained for three days. George refused to have the light on because it hurt his eyes and he sat in bed with the babies by his left side, and smoked.

His daughter Anne had brought the twins. They were eight months old. The boy rested quietly on his back and watched the smoke from the cigarette. George described changing animal shapes in the smoke to the children. The smooth growth of a blue giraffe, the drunken elephant that fell apart, the snakes under water. The girl tried to crawl off the bed and Anne had to hold her.

"Alright, I'll go to Nell's place," George said.

"It'll be good for you, Dad," Anne said. "You should get up and about a bit. I'll take you for walks."

"With all the other old people, eh? That'll be bloody lovely. We'll take some little ham sandwiches."

"Nell will enjoy the company."

"That grumpy old cow? It'll be like being at home when we were kids."

"John said he'd take us down with Anne and the babies," Frieda said.

"If I have to go I want to take my camera," he said. "Still got plenty of shots to take of these two beauties."

He held the boy's small hand and smoked in the

darkening room, the talk of the women as soft as flapping sheets.

The family drove to the sea in the old Morris. George sat in the front seat in his black overcoat with a rug on his knees. Anne's husband drove, and the two women sat in the back with the babies.

The sky was a grey sheet suspended above the bay. The blood red feet of gulls scribbled in the air, and the birds glided and hovered as the car bounced over the rilled Hornibrook Bridge. The wind off the water thudded against the car's doors and windows. Spray dotted the windscreen and George looked through the blur at the sea. At times he thought the white frills on the waves were birds, until they dissolved. It was warm and quiet in the car.

"Used to tear down here on the bikes on Sundays," George said. "Nell never had the kettle on for us, let alone any beer."

"That's because you never told her when you were coming," Frieda said, smiling.

"Women should be ready for things like that."

"Oh, Dad," Anne said. The motion of the car had rocked the babies to sleep.

George smelled salt as the cluster of shops appeared at the end of the bridge. Fibro squares huddled in the wind at the edge of the bay, their walls covered with paintings of grinning blue fish with huge eyes, friendly crabs and sharks.

They usually stopped to buy seafood on their way to Sandgate, but this time they drove past the shops. George turned and watched the bulging fish eyes disappear through the back window.

"They sell good fish here. I remember once when we rode down . . ."

"We'll wait until we get to Nell's," Frieda said.

"You've got to watch what you eat now," Anne said.

He clasped his hands as they coasted down the hill to Nell's house.

Nell's husband brought back sackfulls of shells after his diving trips up north. He travelled to Cairns several times a year where his brother had a wooden sloop, and they would head out to sea in search of pearl.

Although he worked hard it wasn't a job for him, checking air lines and sharpening knives as the deck hand polished his brass diving helmet. He felt a certain freedom sinking to the ocean floor, staggering through seaweed or treading over forests of coral. He gathered beautiful shells because they pleased his wife.

Some of them ended up in her garden at Sandgate. Flower beds were held in place by the chalky palms of clams. And in the house the shells lined shelves and ledges. On a windy day the curtains would flick small ones to the floor, or onto the couch, open magazines, books.

"She's still got the dog's teeth around the garden," George said as the car pulled into the driveway. The wheels crushed old shells that pitted the tyre ruts.

Nell came out onto the back landing, wiping her hands on an apron.

"She's still crazy you know," George said as he stepped out of the car.

"About time you got here," Nell said. "Thought you said you'd be down at two."

"Pipe down girl, we're here aren't we?" George said.

She hugged him and they went into the house. The kettle hissed on the stove, and a sliced bun with lemon icing leaned on its plate in the centre of the kitchen table.

George fell asleep in the brown leather chair near the window in the front room. His head to one side, mouth slightly open.

It was early evening and his grey hair was brilliant white in the glow from the lamp on the television. Nell and Frieda washed the dishes in the kitchen as Anne put the babies to bed. Her husband John had returned to Brisbane for work the next day.

"How's Stan?" Frieda asked.

"Still up in Cairns with Ken," Nell said.

"When will he be back?"

"When he finds enough pearl. That's the usual time."

"We married a couple of wild ones, didn't we?"

"A little too wild sometimes," Nell said. "But you learn to live with it. You have to. You'd know that more than anyone."

Stars appeared above the giant mango tree in the yard. A tree alive with the travel of insects, webs, sap. The tree grew close to the window of the back room where the babies slept. The room, darkened by the shadow of the tree, became part of its murkiness.

The girl slept soundly in the cot. The boy woke, tilted his head back, and watched the scissoring black leaves of the tree through the open window.

"Is Dad all right?" Anne said.

"He's tired from the trip," Frieda said. "It's the furthest he's travelled for a while."

"Does it get cooler later on, Nell? I'm worried about the babies."

"Not this time of year. Even the breeze off the bay is warm."

They had tea and ate the rest of the bun.

"Do you think he has much time, Mum?"

"Who knows what the sea air will do for him. The doctor said if he rested up for a while . . ."

"Mum."

"I don't know love," Frieda said.

They could hear the monotonous call of crickets.

"He'll fight," Nell said. "When he first got his motorcycle he fell off dozens of times. Always got back on it."

Across the street and beyond the vacant lot, trawlers headed out to sea. Their white lights wriggled above the bay.

George stood in shallow water, not far from the shore. The water came up to his knees. He looked down at his brown slippers. Two sleepy fish through the crazed surface of the bay.

"George, what do you think you're doing?" Frieda yelled. "Come back here."

She held her dress between her legs with a bunched fist as the wind toyed at its hem.

"Come on in, the water's fine," he said.

He laughed and then coughed. Spray grazed his brown robe.

It was early morning and George had gone to the shore before the family had woken. He made coffee in

34

the kitchen, smoked a cigarette on the front steps and walked through the vacant lot to the bay.

He walked into the water and it soothed his tender feet. He stood still and imagined being in deeper water, floating, dressed in his old pants with the leather belt, flannelette shirt and slippers. Standing on the ocean floor with a fish passing through his thatch of grey hair.

"You'll get a cold. Come out at once you crazy old man."

The sand began to cover his slippers. He turned and walked out of the water.

"You old fool, what did you do that for?" Frieda said.

"It was fun," he said. His slippers squelched on the hard sand. She began to lead him back to the house.

"I want to look for some shells for the twins," George said. "Bring them down to the beach. And my camera too. It's on the sideboard."

She stood for a moment, watched him weave up the beach, his hands in his pockets, and left.

George carried the small shells in both hands. In the distance he could see his family through the haze, the women forming a crude circle around the babies.

"Have a nice walk, did we?" Nell said, her hands on her hips. "It looks like we'll have to strap you in a chair."

"The doctor said I needed fresh air."

"He didn't say you could go skindiving, did he?" Nell went back to the house.

"She thinks she's my mother," he said. "You all do. I have three mothers now."

He sat on the edge of the blanket and gave the shells to the babies. They played with the gritty objects, bringing them close to their faces, studying the fan of ridges and little caves before dropping them.

He took pictures of the family on the blanket with his old Kodak Brownie. Rested on his elbows for a close-up of the babies and the cream domes of their heads. A grey banner of water stretched behind them and the morning haze, it would show later, fused the ocean and the sky.

It was another warm day at Sandgate. Insects drifted in the heat above the grass. Blades and stalks sweated vivid green. Bees swivelled around flowers, garden clams, and the bulk of the mango tree next to the house.

George sat in his chair in the front room. He felt like he was floating in clear water. It was cool in the house and around his feet, through the fibre of his slippers and the white bone of his ankles. The space between his curved spine and the backrest of the chair felt especially cold. It would be nice in the water of the bay, he thought. Silent in the blue water. The swaying fishing lines of the children on the pier. Steel hooks and worms on newspapers.

Anne had been gone for a week. She took the twins back to Brisbane and promised to return. They left in a silver bus that wheezed to Nell's back gate. George stood on the concrete verandah and waved. Anne propped the babies up to the bus window, grimy from the breaths of weekday schoolchildren, and smiled.

It was a dim, wriggling portrait. The girl pushed away from the glass but the boy stayed and saw the waving hands. Flickering fingers through the leaves of trees as the bus edged away.

George heard the motor of the bus strain as it went

over the hill. Saliva from the babies' kisses was cool on his cheek in the breeze.

He sat in the chair and thought about the babies. The cigarette pack, on the cane table next to the chair, was full. His fresh coffee was steaming and he opened the new cigarettes. He put the cellophane, still shaped the square of the packet, into the ashtray. There were two terrier dogs on the side of the black ashtray. An advertisement for Scotch whisky. The dogs were filthy. The white dog's hair was tinged with the yellow of nicotine. The black dog was spotted with ash. He pulled out the silver paper in the packet and it scraped over the face of the long white cigarettes. He took one slowly from the pack and listened to its papery withdrawal. The cigarettes moved. Pressure eased. He lit the cigarette and drew in the smoke, then blew it out in white columns through his nostrils. The smoke splayed and became thin. Through this he watched his wife and sister weeding around the front letterbox.

They kneeled on the grass at the base of the brown post, the tin letterbox screwed to its top. Both had scarves around their hair. They giggled and chattered in the warm air, pulling weeds from under the clam shells around the post. Shells stained with red dirt. The women's knees were the colour of the earth.

Cigarette ash floated onto his hands, the chair's armrest, the buttons of his shirt. He had finished one-third of the cigarette.

It was so quiet he could hear the air rushing through the channels of his throat. The tin roof crackled. He thought he could hear the mango tree, the pressing of fibre in its gnarled trunk. Fruit pushing out from the seeds.

He drew on the cigarette and the smoke slid into his nose and mouth, around his teeth and over his tongue. The cigarette was half-finished.

George felt the pain, as deep as a vibration in the mango tree roots. Cold pain, and the heat outside a shifting of black patches, spots, mesh. He sank back in the chair, one slipper suspended above the floor, the other planted against the boards. The women outside faded and reappeared in sharp detail. Their talk drifted in and out, stopped, started, and the cigarette in his right hand ran through his fingers, the ash tumbling in minute arcs as it fell to the floor, the smoke tangled. The cigarette rolled between the floorboards and scorched the wood. It burned out, leaving a fragile skeleton of ash, and George looked out the window to the clear sky.

*

The house by the bay is gone. I travelled down to Sandgate in a long, silver-ribbed coach, over the new concrete bridge that runs beside the buckled Hornibrook, past the fibro fish and chip shops with whitewashed sides and ghostly crabs staring through the thin layers of paint, and down to the edge of the bay to find the house had disappeared.

The mango tree still stood in the yard. It looked smaller than when I saw it as a boy on holidays. Its nutty trunk flecked with white, as if shells had grown into the bark. A plastic swing with nylon ropes dangled from its limbs.

I stood on the footpath next to the fence and tried to draw out the old house's angles and colours and dimensions from the salt air. In its place stood a perfectly square, tan brick house with sliding windows and floral curtains. White pipes ran down the side of the house and into the ground. A concrete driveway led into an open garage filled with paint cans, brushes, bicycle tubes, jars of nails, bags of fertiliser and a child's canoe.

For a moment I felt the old house was still there. Maybe pressed inside the new house, or just over the other side of the green tiled roof. I went around to the front yard, its grass neatly clipped and bordered by a grey wire fence. In the corner, under a shrub, was one of Aunt Nell's old clam shells, streaked with red soil stains.

I had twenty minutes before the bus arrived and went down to the jetty. I loved going there as a child, its bleached planks, rusted bolt heads and wooden pylons too big to put your arms around. Burnt at the top like dead matches. I dangled my feet over the edge and, because the tide was so high, could dip my running shoes in the water.

My family had told me the house was no longer there. That it had been torn down, the cracked fibro sheets, floorboards and tin taken away by men in trucks. Maybe children had crawled over mountains of rubbish at the nearby tip, at dusk, and dragged home pieces of the house for their billy-carts, or secret cubbies beneath the earth. But I still had to come back and see for myself.

As I headed home, I knew my grandfather was even further away. Seeing the new house on the old piece of land, it was as if a link to him had also been demolished. Now I was left with my own childhood memories of the place. And I wondered what road had to be torn up, what storm had to come and claim the old jetty, what more had to be built before they, too, were lost.

The Motorcycle Cafe

Whenever George worked under a car with his silver wrench, he thought of poetry. He saw the feathery heads of weeds stuck between black pipes. Flowers caught around axles. Even ladybirds trapped in patches of grease. He recited all these things to me. I worked under the bonnet and he whispered his poetry up through radiators and cylinder heads.

George and I worked as a team in a small garage. My real name was Dave, but everyone called me Rev. It wasn't short for a priest or holy person or anything like that. It was because I liked fast cars, and motorcycles. We had been together for many years, and in the early days he came to work in his blue overalls. He usually brought his notebook and pen. I could pick them. They bulged from the pocket over his thigh like funny shaped muscles, warm all day from the heat of his leg.

He didn't want me to tell anyone about the notebook. I guess he was worried about what the other mechanics might think about him and his poetry. He showed it to me a couple of times. He drew really well. Lots of women around the blocks of words. Glamorous girls with words written right across their chests. Some had fullstops and commas on their arms.

I remember George sitting out in the wreck in that cold stony yard with all the smashed car bodies, and the rest of us eating corned meat sandwiches and sipping hot coffee in the lunch room. On other days he would be just like the rest of us without a thought for poetry. He made steaming mugs of coffee for everyone and we moved our chairs into a circle and talked, mostly about women, tools, and what nice coffee George made.

He was liked by all the other mechanics and he worked very hard. Even when it was cold and the tools were almost too painful to touch, George worked hard. He enjoyed fixing cars with his strong hands. When he held wrenches they were weapons. But when he held that fine nib pen over his notebook, he could have been a craftsman making a glass bird, or repairing a watch.

I think George's contrasts confused a lot of people. I called them his gears. People met him at the pub some evenings and he'd be surrounded by men who talked and joked and bought him beer. They loved to hear George talk. On other nights he wanted me to sit with him at a corner table. He would just sit and spill tobacco on the wooden table, pushing it around with his forefinger and telling me it reminded him of the fields beyond the village. It was the only reason he carried a packet of tobacco, he said, because it was like having his own private field in his pocket. George, he had many gears.

The Radiator Inn was our favourite, and George saw many of his sketches there. We drank beer and stared at all the women with yellow ringlets and white faces. George never went too close to those sorts of women. He watched them, like the rest of us, but he kept away from what he called the danger of their glamour. I quite liked them and bought them drinks until they forgot about my grease-stained hands.

41

After too many beers we walked home. All the lights of the village twinkled and George called the world a soft black evening dress. Then he would go quiet and I talked while he nodded. When I reached my house I said goodnight and he said the same. I stood in my front garden with cold plant leaves touching my arms and watched George walk off and disappear. Just like the movie I saw, when the man walked into the ocean.

*

"Rev," George would say to me, "let's go down to my favourite little cafe by the sea."

The little cafe by the sea was George's name for the gymnasium. It was a square building made of wooden slats, iron and glass. We walked down the road to the beach, instead of going to the Radiator, and we could see the gym down on the sand like a washed up crate.

After working all day in the garage George and I loved to sit on the sand and watch the sea. The waves were mauve in the late afternoon. Large cream shells littered the shore and I laughed every time George called it the Beach of Human Ears. He had a name for everything.

After a while we went into the gymnasium. It was what I imagined being underwater was like. It had a wall of glass that faced the sea, and opposite it was another wall covered in mirrors. When sunlight bounced off the small waves the sea swirled in the gymnasium. George told me to look at the shadows of training men moving around the green room like sharks.

George changed into his gym clothes — long white baggy trousers and a singlet with circles cut from the sides to show his muscles. All the men had them on. I sat in the corner on a stool and watched them straining their muscles in the fading light.

After an hour of lifting weights George sat with me in front of the glass wall and we talked. Sweat beaded on his forehead. We spoke about work, motorcycles, and his sketching. He explained how he drew all those girls from the pubs, their dreamy eyes and red lips. He said all the sketches came from memory. He didn't like to draw something in front of him. He preferred scenes from a short past, he said.

"It is like," George said, "watching the sea through the salty glass of the gymnasium."

*

Often we walked to Joe's Garage for supper after the gymnasium. George marvelled at the rows of cottages as ordered as back knuckles up that road from the beach, the gardens full of flowers and the warm glow of lamps.

All his dreams fell along the road at night, like the moths that struck the hot glass of the streetlights. He dreamed out loud in a sad voice. I always counted on our get-together with Joe to lift his spirits.

George always said that Joe's Garage looked tired from the outside. The wood was old and slate grey. A dusty yellow sign hung above the front windows. Down the side of the building were huge weeds and forgotten motor parts. This was our territory, George's and mine. Lots of parts and grease and coffee.

Joe was always there. The "motorcycle maniac" as George called him. You could hardly see him squatting amongst the thousands of parts that littered the floor and covered the walls.

"Hello George, Rev," he said. Joe had a cigarette in his mouth and was fixing a motorcycle. When he worked on a cycle he seemed to become attached to the machine, like a fleshy side mirror or an extra foot pedal. That's what George said anyway. That Joe was married to his machines.

George made the coffee. He loved drinking and making it. I must admit I never tasted better coffee. He made it like no other person, even though he just used coffee, milk and sugar like everyone else. Joe swore he never made himself a cup during the day because it never tasted as good as George's cups at night.

"Will you join me in the sitting room, chaps," George said jokingly when the coffee was ready. We retreated to the corner of the garage. Hundreds of small black parts had been pushed back to make room for a thick rug covered with dirty rose and leaf patterns. There were also three old chairs, a coffee table and a glass ashtray or two. As George said, it was like sitting in the middle of a forest.

Even though we talked for hours and drank coffee until our bellies were tight, you could feel a sort of loneliness in the garage. I walked to the wooden outhouse, past a few wrecks and over the cold stone ground and the loneliness was there, too.

When the coffee and talk stopped, or the cigarettes ran out, we said goodnight to Joe. He always yelled out the same thing as we walked down the side of the garage, past the tall weeds.

"George," Joe said, "you should go into business making coffee for the whole world."

*

Saturday was the big day for trying out cafes. George came around to my house on his black Matchless. He

44

wore black leather pants and a jacket. He also had a headpiece made of leather, and round fighter pilot goggles. He stood on my front lawn and looked like a wrinkled seal. He always carried the same dirty old tourist map in his chest pocket.

I rode a Matchless similar to George's, and we would cruise through the village, side by side, and leave behind the tight winding streets for the fields and open roads. At every stop we made, George told me how the ride felt. He seemed to feel every little detail. He said the roads through the fields were gentle, and he imagined he was riding his motorcycle over a row of whales, all head to tail. The landscape swam through his goggles. The cows that dotted the fields were like brown cars, he said, their sides scratched by the wildflowers. He felt every leaf and branch and stone on the road when he pressed his feet down hard on the pedals and pulled up on the handlebars.

We rode until we reached the first cafe for the day. I particularly remember the cafe in the green filling station not far from the village. George said he could almost smell the coffee through the cafe windows and feel the cold curve of the white saucers.

We sat in a booth and ordered coffee and cake. The waitress wore a frilly blouse. When she held her order pad level with our faces I could smell the onions and hamburger meat soaked into her hands. The grease of her trade, George remarked. A food mechanic.

"Think of all the notebooks these girls go through," George said when the waitress left us. "All full of food scribbles. Page after page of figures and doodles."

The coffee arrived. George took one sip and pushed the cup aside. It tasted like a paper napkin, he said. A girl spoke to a boy in the next booth, the sound of her voice as annoying as a distant radio. Her lipstick smudged with every mouthful of food. I drank my coffee and ate the dry cake.

George refused to finish the cake so we left in search of a nicer, cleaner, tastier cafe, started our Matchless cycles and roared off into the hills, leaving George's half-eaten cake on a saucer at the empty booth.

*

Elaine sat by the window in her front room, behind a lace curtain, and looked down into the street. She sat on a brown chair covered with a pattern of leaves. Every Saturday afternoon she waited for George.

Of all the girls he knew, she was the only one he ever showed any real interest in. He talked about her at the garage, and called her his little china baby. George said her skin was as pure as a white china cup.

After our Saturday rides she was there waiting for him. He lived down the corridor from her in a boarding house, and sometimes she cooked him meals. Every Saturday it was roast lamb with a cold bottle of beer.

She worked for the local gas company in a large office with a huge cardboard flame advertisement that stood in the window facing the street. She sat at a typewriter in the shadow of the flame. All day she typed and filed with those girls of the pubs who talked about the night before, and the men smelling of beer in dark cars later on. When it wasn't men they spoke about diamond rings, dresses, hairpins. They giggled as they worked.

At night the office girls walked home or to the pubs in their gas blue uniforms and white shoes. Elaine never went to the pubs. She went back to the boarding house and sometimes George would have coffee with her. I had coffee with them both some nights. Elaine looked a bit out of place sitting in George's room, on a chair draped with dirty singlets and shirts. Small even surrounded by his sketches of blue factories, birds, hills, roads and motors.

When we were alone George tried to explain Elaine's beauty to me. He always tried to explain such things to me, as if I had no mind of my own. I thought those women at the pubs with their lovely bright lips, wavy hair and perfume were beautiful, but he said I didn't understand beauty.

There was nothing in the surface beauty of women who knew how to draw well with thick nibs of lipstick and eye pencils, he said. Elaine's beauty came from somewhere behind her face. It could be found in the down on her neck when her hair was pinned up, in the curve of a cheek or the sadness of eyes looking downwards. I let him think what he liked.

He sketched Elaine once. She was sitting on his Matchless and leaning forward, as if she was riding. The motorcycle was drawn down to the last detail in black ink. He even put in the stitching on the leather seat, and reflections in the chrome. But Elaine was drawn in a soft and delicate way with just a few strokes of the pen.

He gave it to her and she pinned it to her sitting room wall, above the sideboard. Elaine put it where she could see it from her chair when she waited for him on a Saturday afternoon. When she heard the roar of our motorcycles streets away, she started carving the meat.

It was a nice set-up that George had, coming home to a lovely woman and a hot meal. But George was not a man for routines. When his work or people started crowding in on him he just jumped on that black Matchless and rode. When he couldn't ride, he sketched. George was no routine man, and I wondered how long he would last with his china baby.

I think it was about 3am on a Monday when George rang me. We had been to Joe's place for drinks the night before. I remember it because it was the day George's mother had died, and we drank a lot in silence. He was devastated. He just kept saying he had to get away. He spoke quickly on the telephone that morning. He said he wanted to leave the garage, the gymnasium, the village, everything. He asked if I would come with him. I said yes so I could go back to bed and sleep off my hangover. He said something about finding the perfect place where he could start again. I went to sleep and dreamt of a huge red cafe full of tables and chairs that were carved out of dirt, and saucers covered with leaves.

*

So we ended up in this tropical town where the post office and cathedrals and libraries were made of sandstone blocks, with the green statue of a Queen on the edge of a park, pigeons and palm trees and gritty afternoon dust, a river spanned by a spider metal bridge, houses up on stumps, plenty of heat, flies and a big clock in the middle of town, all on the other side of the world.

George was the type of person that could get other people caught up in his enthusiasm and carry them off before they knew what had happened. That's what happened to me, and I wondered if I had done the right thing, sitting in an old wooden house we had rented with big leafy plants knodding against the low-set windows. I had sold my Matchless. I only had a small bag of clothes with me. I watched storms roll over the hills, almost every night. The rain was so heavy it made all the plants

48

and trees shake. Steam hung over bitumen roads, like it did on the surface of George's coffee.

We got jobs as mechanics and worked around as a team for a few months before George rented an old disused store in a suburb near a brewery. Standing on the footpath outside the store, I could smell malt in the air.

"This is it," George said, showing me through the store, its window at the front cream with dust. "I'll work at the front with the leathers, and you'll be out back with the motorcycles."

It was to be a motorcycle shop. I was back where I started, working on the cycles, and George was moving onto new ground, stitching leather, making jackets, boots and gloves. He said he wanted to save the skin of men from the inevitable fall. It was one of the sketches over again, I thought. The hard mechanics at the back, the oil, wrenches and fumes, and the soft leather at the front. Like Elaine on the Matchless, or just watching the sea after work.

We cleaned up the shop and the shed out the back where I was to work. George did the signwriting himself on a plywood sheet, and hoisted it above the red tin awning that stretched out over the footpath in front of the shop. I must admit it was a beautiful sign. He had painted a yellow field, violet mountains and a black motorcycle, a Matchless, in the foreground. This was home, nailed up on our shop.

George worked late at night with his leather and made some nice things. The day the shop opened an old woman came in looking for a handbag, and a dog peered briefly into the strange smelling store. George sat there all day, surrounded by his black leather.

At the end of the day he locked the front door and came around to the shed where I was cleaning some parts. He sat and said nothing, and in the end it was up to me to make the coffee. George drank it but I knew it tasted awful. I made better cups of tea.

*

It was either the local motorcycle club or those American movies about rebels and gangs that screened at the Plaza that was the saviour of our business. Men started arriving at the shop, growling their cycles and parking them on an angle in front of the red awning like they were horses outside a saloon. They were keen motorcyclists who talked about racing, spark plugs, helmets, leathers. They crowded around each other's cycles and looked over the machines.

George invited them in and they all sat around on crates and on the floor and laughed and talked as George brought them coffee and I knew that was it, that we would never get rid of them. They were an investment, George said, and he was right. Before long the clubs bought the leathers they needed from George, brought the difficult repairs to me, and drank lots of coffee.

Then things began to change. I was still stuck out the back with the grime, the tools hanging from nails on the shed wall, the sink in the corner. But out the front, George began to move a few things around. The leather jackets and gloves were taken away from the window and hung or placed neatly on new racks and shelves that he had built behind the counter.

George met a girl. She was the niece of one of the men in the motorcycle club. He took her to the Plaza on the back of his new motorcycle. She loved grabbing onto his leather jacket and flying around the streets.

Chairs appeared in the store. Old wooden kitchen chairs. I said to George, why do we need all these ridiculous chairs, no motorcycle garage ever had so many silly chairs, and he said quietly, we have no ordinary motorcycle garage here, and the chairs are important if men are going to relax and talk cycles. Relax and talk cycles. I slaved away out the back, my fingers and knuckles barked, with headaches from the sound of engines, and he wanted to relax and talk.

That was when he was happiest, talking and drinking with lots of men, crowds of them. The motorcycle clubs even began to hold their meetings in our shop every Tuesday and Thursday nights. They spent hours organising races, outings, trophies.

"What we have here is an important shop," George said to me. A serious motorcycle shop. I began to get less jobs and sat in my shed listening to my old ivory-coloured radio that was covered in grease and thumb prints. The constant crowds in the front ruined my evenings with Glenn Miller and Jack Benny.

This was the George I knew of the Saturday morning cafes. George searching for that perfect place where the surroundings and tastes and people all clicked at once. But there was no place like this, I told George. Something was always wrong or out of step. The cake would be too dry or the laminex tables would have somebody's old coffee rings on them. One of those many pure white cups always had a chip or fracture. I will find it one day, George said, and if I don't find it, I'll make it.

Sitting out the back in my shed with my shoes up and listening to those beautiful trumpets on the radio, I thought maybe George was doing just that, trying to create his perfect place.

*

It was five years before I returned to the motorcycle shop George and I started. I left because there were no repairs after a while. Everything seemed to have been sucked into the front of that old store, right into the leather smells and talk. I worked as a mechanic in another suburb and married a girl I met at a pub. I asked her to marry me one Saturday afternoon, standing at the bar that smelled of stale beer, with cigarette smoke everywhere and me in my dirty overalls, and she said yes.

From a long way down the street, through the insect filth of my Zephyr windscreen, I saw that black Matchless in the yellow fields on George's sign. The sign was dull, like the rest of the suburb. The Plaza had shut down and the foyer was used for monthly citizens meetings. The printing shop was full of ferns and garden manuals. Other buildings had disappeared.

I parked the car where all those motorcycles used to be, and looked through the front glass of the shop. A side window was smashed. The counter was still there and George's racks and shelves. There were a couple of broken chairs in a heap.

George lived down the road, within sight of that Matchless. It was Saturday afternoon, all lazy with heat, and I could hear the races being called on a radio somewhere.

Parking in front of George's little fibro house felt strange. It was like the days when we would coast into the cafes, over the smooth bitumen past the petrol bowsers, or into a car park. The road in front of his house was very smooth and covered in black tyre marks.

The house was high on stumps, and underneath was George's workshop. He was standing at his bench when I walked across the front lawn. The grass was trampled and oily. He saw me and smiled in the way that attracted so many people. He talked and joked, made me coffee, and we sat downstairs on two cane chairs next to an enormous Buick with four flat tyres. He said he was still fixing it up.

He told me he was working more with his commercial art, and that he had built a motorcycle helmet a few years ago that was proved at the time to be the safest in the world. From a drawer in his workbench he produced a photograph of a ute balanced on four of his helmets.

He married that girl who loved riding on his motorcycle and they had a daughter. He got more photographs from the drawer. We had another cup of coffee and at the far end of the workbench I noticed the wall of Nescafe tins. Not small tins but big catering size, and they were all lined up perfectly with the labels facing outwards.

I stayed for dinner and George's wife was very nice. She worked away in the kitchen, walking back and forth to the dining room, bringing new dishes and cups, jelly, cream, fruit, coffee and George's favourite yellow cake. She made good cake and I ate quite a few pieces as George and I talked about the business of signwriting.

Then I heard the noises. A humming sound until I heard revving and backfires, and I knew there were motorcycles approaching. George turned his head slightly to the side and smiled.

"It's the boys," he said, "back from the races."

We went to the front door and stood on the wooden landing. In they came, dozens of motorcycles ridden by men in black and brown leather jackets. They parked everywhere, in George's flower garden, on the footpath, in front and behind my star blue Zephyr, under the front stairs, beneath the poinsettia tree. I had never seen so many cycles in such a small area.

"I'd better get the coffee on," George said, and I

realised nothing had changed with him. The men came thundering up the front stairs, chairs were rearranged and tables pushed to the sides. I spoke to some of the men but all they wanted to talk about was cycles, which didn't interest me any more. One of the men, Jack, had a fresh graze on his cheek.

George's wife was better than any waitress I had seen in those many cafes. She filled cup after cup, brought cake and biscuits, and then more coffee. All the men were talking at once and I could see George was happy. He spoke quickly like an excited child.

I went into the kitchen where George's daughter, Anne, was trying to do some homework at the kitchen table. She drew possums and fruit bats in an exercise book. Frieda was washing cups then drying them for the next round of coffee. She told me she used to be a waitress at Coles, serving hot food during winter to all the people from the big offices, and then she had to get on her hands and knees after the cafeteria had closed and scrub the day's filth from the floor.

"I never minded that," Frieda said, "but now I'm doing it all again at home." She smiled but nothing here was funny. Steam puffed from a kettle on the gas stove. She rushed with coffee into the room of men.

I stood by the kitchen louvres and looked out into the backyard. There were no motorcycles on the grass, only dry pods from a massive poinciana tree and a wooden toy aeroplane. George had built the plane for his daughter. It needed a new coat of white paint.

"This place," Frieda said, laughing and pinning a loose wave of hair behind her ear, "this place is like a cafe sometimes. A motorcycle cafe."

I said goodbye to George and his wife and they walked me to the Zephyr. Some of the men had to be called to move their motorcycles because the car was blocked in. The men waved goodbye, some wearing gloves, some not, and I drove past the Matchless shop one more time on the way home to my family.

*

George was dead. His wife rang me and told me he died of cancer of the bladder. I hadn't seen him for years and now old George was dead. Fit George who used to work out at the gymnasium and walk home with arms of stone. George, the man who made the strongest motorcycle helmet in the world. Now he was gone. She asked me to come to the funeral and I said I'd try and make it.

I had no intention of going and seeing all those black cycles following the coffin in a car full of flowers, or leading the hearse to the crematorium and parking on that immaculate grass, dripping oil.

Poor old George, thinking those cycles would take him to that perfect place one day. Those bits of metal and paint and oil that get old like people and break down like people too. Poor old George thinking that.

*

I've just read an interesting article in a magazine about coffee and how it might be the cause of cancer, cancer of the bladder, and I think of George and his wall of coffee tins, George passing blood for ages and not telling anyone, like that little notebook only I knew about, and wonder if coffee could have been the death of George. Just in case, I tell my wife we are to drink no more coffee in our house, no more Nescafe or International Roast, just tea. We only drink tea in our house now.

The White Aeroplane

I burned the white aeroplane years ago, in the rusty tin drum in the corner of the yard under the giant poinciana tree. It lay in pieces under George's workbench for ages so I decided to get rid of it.

It made me feel sad feeding my husband's plane into the fire. George had worked so hard on that toy plane. He built it for our daughter Anne, and spent months painting and polishing it until it was as smooth as glass. Then he took it apart when she got older and he got older, and it turned pale yellow over the years under the bench. Until I burned it, and it turned black.

George started the plane when I was pregnant with Anne. He said he was going to build his child a flying machine that would take her wherever she wanted to go. To the sea, over the mountains, or even to exotic places in history. His plane would have no respect for time, he said.

I was cooking lamb and vegetables for lunch one Saturday. Through the louvres and down into the backyard I could see George with wood he bought for the plane. Some of the strips of wood were thick, and others thin, placed across his two paint-spattered trestles. He checked the wood carefully and ran his hands in circular motions with the grain.

The following week he drew the plans for the aeroplane. He sat in the kitchen in the evenings with his cigarettes and his black-rimmed glasses and drew on large white sheets of butchers' paper he had got from Les down the road.

I sat at the table and knitted booties as he covered the paper in lines and figures. He used a fat blue pencil that he held like a cigarette when he was thinking. He drew quickly, the aeroplane a flat blue shape on the paper. The night he finished the plans he sat me on a chair next to him and went through the sketches from start to finish.

The aeroplane looked lovely, even on the creased sheets of paper. It had an open cockpit. Each wing had a single propeller. There were wheels below the seat. The whole plane would be mounted on a stand a few feet high.

In the drawings George had even sketched a little child. Not a boy or a girl, but a figure with simple dot eyes and a smiling mouth. I hugged him and he grabbed me by the waist and gazed over the plans. I never realised until much later how badly he wanted to be that stick child.

*

George was painting planes at the nearby Airforce base when I gave birth to Anne. He didn't go to war because he had flat feet, and used his signwriting skills on bombers that probably never left the base.

He arrived at the hospital late in the afternoon. I

remember him standing at the end of my bed and smiling, with a cigarette in his mouth. The cigarette lifted slightly and smoke curled from the end.

A nurse showed him his new daughter, then he came back and sat on the edge of the bed. His weight forced my left leg towards him.

"We did well, didn't we?" he said.

"Yes, we did," I said, and reached out for his hand.

"I'll have to get moving on that plane."

"Yes, she'll be grown up before we know it."

Back at home, I often went to bed early. I could hear the slice of his chisel as I rested on my back on the sagging bed. He worked firstly on the propellers. I imagined him making them like they do with tiny model aeroplanes, just flat but shaped like propellers. But he carved them out of a single piece of timber, the same way as the genuine plane-makers. It was as if he was shaping the plane so it could really fly.

When he worked I could smell cigarette smoke coming up through the bedroom floorboards. The light from his workshop bulb crept through the cracks as well, and if I looked down next to the rug I could see lines of pale yellow.

At the same time every night he sat and drank his coffee and smoked cigarettes. He had a small flask with a dulled silver lid which he filled with coffee before he went downstairs. It held exactly two cups and he drank them both, sitting in the cane chair next to the bench.

During the day I looked after Anne and tidied George's bench and work area. He finished the propellers after a few months and wrapped them tightly in plastic. He leaned them in one corner of his darkroom. The wheels were also done and the work on the main body was half-finished. The plane rested on the two spindly trestles and looked like a strange creamy fish.

One day I decided to clean out his bench drawers, pulled one from its slot and placed it on the sketches on top of the bench. It was full of tools, rulers, pencils, sheets of sandpaper, tacks, rolls of film and some photographs of his friends riding motorcycles. And right at the back of the drawer, in between the pages of an old nurse's handbook, were some letters.

George's name was written on the front of the blue envelopes in what I knew was a woman's hand. I decided not to open them and put them back in the drawer. A small picture fell from between the letters. It was of a young George with a girl dressed in a school uniform. They were sitting on the corner of a blanket spread on the ground. She looked thin in the tunic, with a long neck and dark lips. Her hair was black and in a bob.

I replaced the drawer then went upstairs and checked on Anne. After that I made a pot of tea and sat at the kitchen table, thinking about the letters. Blue letters and wood shavings, that was all I could think of.

*

The finished plane was wheeled out under a thick grey blanket on Anne's second birthday. Relatives had been invited over for the unveiling so George set up some tables downstairs, near the tail end of the old Buick he bought from a man called Smithy.

I covered the odd tables with floral tablecloths and put out sandwiches and cake. The chairs were all different too, gathered from the bathroom, kitchen, dining room and other parts of the house. And when my family and some of George's friends sat around the tables they looked like children themselves, some perched on stools and enjoying the height, and others sunk low with their chins level with my pink sand cakes.

Anne sat in a wooden high-chair at the head of the tables. When George pushed the plane out from the side of the Buick everyone sighed and smiled and looked at Anne. She saw everyone else with their mouths wide open and began to giggle.

The aeroplane stand wheels squeaked as they rolled across the concrete. George looked at her and grinned. At the same time he pinched both sides of the blanket and flicked it high into the air like a magician. The white aeroplane burst out, as if from the side of a storm cloud.

It was a beautiful piece of work. A long, white plane that was so shiny it reflected light and gravel, even the shoes of the visitors, on its undercarriage. It was cocked slightly to the left on the wooden stand, its two black wooden wheels ready to grip any runway. The cockpit was padded in rich maroon-coloured leather, stretched tight with gold-headed tacks. George had painted an instrument panel of flat dashes and figures. It looked like it could fly, but in all the years we owned the white aeroplane it rarely left the airspace under the house.

The men inspected the work, ran their hands along its smooth surface, gently spun the wheels and crouched down to look under the wings.

"It's a lovely plane, George," they all said. And it was. It was soothing to look at and flowed back in curves and angles as if in flight.

George took Anne in his arms and lowered her into the cockpit. She looked small in the leather seat, her blonde hair even lighter against the leather. She sat quietly and peered through the tiny glass windscreen.

"Now you're as free as a bird, Annie," he said, spinning the wooden propellers. She laughed at the whir the propellers made and looked over at the women at the tables. They smiled at Anne, their heads to one side like the aeroplane itself, and ate the pink cake.

*

The letters kept appearing. They never turned up in our tin letterbox out the front. They were addressed to George but care of his mate Jack who lived a suburb away beside the brewery.

I checked the drawer several times over the next few months and strained my eyes peering into the cracks between the bedroom floorboards at night. Sometimes he looked up and I froze. Then he just lowered his head and smoked in his usual rhythmic way.

Downstairs was George's lonely world. It was not a sad type of loneliness, but one that he enjoyed. He always said he had to have time to himself. He had his darkroom downstairs as well. I had only been in there a few times and never touched anything. It was his own little place. He had the workbench, his cane chairs, his thermos, his motorcycle he called Satan, and the old Buick. And he had the white aeroplane.

He loved going down there at night to work with wood or leather, and I suppose to be close to his secret letters. He must have felt a sort of freedom, sitting in the dim light and looking out into the street. Maybe he was flying in the white aeroplane across the night sky.

*

Anne became too big to sit in the aeroplane. It only took a year before she became cramped in the cockpit, her legs pressed up against the dash and her knees blocking the pilot's view.

But she was still attracted to that wooden toy. When she didn't squeeze herself into it she draped a blanket over its wings and made a cubby house. At night, when her father worked on leather jackets or motorcycle helmets at his bench, she played with dolls in the gloom under the aeroplane. When she was far too old for cubby houses and started going out with boys, the plane was gradually pushed into the corner.

It seemed to move itself over the years, inch by inch, to the outside edge of the workshop. George had his back to the plane most of the time, and it became a haven for mice and sometimes homeless cats.

At some stage George even used it as extra bench space. I saw nuts and bolts, boxes of nails and a handsaw resting on its creamy wings. Once he balanced an empty coffee cup on the plane's tail but I removed the cup before it shattered on the concrete.

I told George to dump the plane but he refused. He was attached to that old thing and it remained motionless in the cool dark under the house.

*

George carefully took the plane apart and stored it under his bench when Anne married the Catholic boy. He never even tried to restore it, as he did most things. It laid in a neat bundle, the pieces strapped tightly together with strips of leather. The paint was dull and the wooden joins were exposed to the dust.

One Saturday George was working on a pot plant stand for me. He bought some special soft pine and was shaping a piece in the lathe when I brought him his morning coffee and biscuits. We sat in the cane chairs and watched steam coming off the road after a sudden downpour of rain. The whole workshop was filled with the smell of soil.

"If it turns out can you make my sister one?" I said.

"If she wants one," he said.

"And Anne might like one in her new house."

"Yeah."

I looked over beneath the bench and saw the pile that was the aeroplane.

"Maybe you should fix up that plane," I said. "You never know when the grandchildren might come along."

He sipped the coffee and stared out at the street. I could see the lines of his face in the dull light. I only noticed his aging in stages, if I stopped and concentrated. His hair was going grey, as if from the inside out. And his skin had a greyish tinge from the smoking.

"What do you think?" I asked.

"The wood is too old," he said, snapping a biscuit with his teeth.

"Buy some new wood. You could make another one couldn't you?"

He looked at the old plane. One side of his face was in shadow and his eyes were moist. He looked at it for a long time and I knew how special it was to him, as if he had sealed a little of himself beneath its surface.

"I don't know whether I could. It's a big job."

"It would be nice for Anne and John. They'd be thrilled."

He shook his head.

"You could start work on it now and who knows, it might be ready in time for some grandchildren," I said.

"That's a big risk to take," George said.

"You like risks."

"I guess I do."

*

He set to work on a new aeroplane. He dug up the original plans from a drawer in the darkroom and started to work on the body. The new project excited him and he even looked healthier.

But it looked out of time now, the plane. We had been living with television for a while and the world, green through our fibreglass magnifier, changed. Cars were smaller. Men no longer wore hats. People travelled through the air in helicopters.

Months later, when George was working on the propellers, I got a phone call from Anne. She was pregnant. I ran halfway down the back stairs and I leaned down next to a stump.

"Your daughter is going to have a baby," I yelled.

There was silence except for the clicking of wood on wood from the propeller George was spinning on a peg in the vice.

He hooted with joy and then he was gone. He left the propeller spinning. I found out later he had gone to tell his friends from the motorcycle club. And he bought some new leather for the cockpit of the plane from the store.

*

George had fitted the wings by the time Anne had the twins. The wings were long, light brown and smooth. He spent hours sanding them back and getting them perfect. He had fine wood shavings in his hair when he went up to the hospital to see the babies for the first time.

It was very early one Monday morning and the roads to the hospital were still damp with dew. George laughed, whistled and joked all the way. Although he was happy I knew he was not well and that he was trying to hide the pain.

We went up to Anne's ward and waited near the nurse's desk. George looked around at the white curtains, the steel piping over the beds, people tucked under sheets, the fruit on the tables and the cut-glass jugs of water. He looked tired enough to be in one of the beds himself, wearing his baggy pants and scuffed brown shoes which were still a little damp from walking on the wet grass at home. Small poinciana leaves were stuck to the leather.

He was quiet. When I held his hand he smiled.

"A boy and a girl in one go," I said.

"She always was a bloody clever little one, my Anne," George said.

"You'll have to put another seat in the aeroplane."

"It's too late."

"No it's not," I said. "It'll just take a bit of extra work."

"It's too late," he said, staring at the rows of white beds.

The nurse took us to the viewing room. We stood in front of the glass and looked at several babies in square cribs on long steel legs. The nurse wheeled our two babies over to the window.

Many other people had stood in front of the window before because there were dozens of fingerprints on the glass where they had tried to reach out and touch the babies in the room. Our grand-daughter was asleep and although she was small, the boy was smaller. His legs were as thin as pencils and his head as big as a bunched fist. His eyes were closed and he was kicking up at us the whole time, struggling in that crib.

George lightly put his fingers on the window ledge and looked at the babies. He couldn't stop grinning, looking from one to the other.

"They're small, aren't they?" he said.

"Yes."

"They're smaller than any of the others."

After a while the nurses took them away. We saw Anne and then went home. I made a pot of tea and George and I sat on the front steps in the sun. Sparrows skipped across the lawn and it was quiet except for their peeps and the sound of cars heading for the city.

"We're grandparents you know," George said after a while.

*

George never finished the second aeroplane. He died when the children were eight months old, and the incomplete plane was left standing under the house with his tools around its base. Near it were two unopened cans of white paint.

After he died his friends and relatives took a lot of his machinery, tools and other belongings from under the house when I was away at my sister's place. My brother took the half-finished plane and used the wood for odd jobs.

As for the letters, they turned up years later. By then they were just pieces of paper. He had taken with him their importance.

Now I think about the first white aeroplane more and more, and the colour of the flames when I fed it piece by piece into the fire. It was hard to burn that old yellow paint, so thick and tight around the wood. But for a while the flames were the most exquisite blue in that rusted open drum in the corner of the yard.

Weddings: The Guest

I hate wearing my thick dark suit. I have to, for Frieda. I hang it in the brown wooden cupboard with the hole punched in its front door. George always says to me, "Jack, mate, the day you wear a bloody suit we'll be burying you." We're a lot alike, George and I.

I bought the suit years ago for a funeral. A fat woman in the second-hand shop had to take a pair of trousers from one hanger and a coat from another because I have big shoulders. I was pretty lucky the top and bottom were almost the same colour. I leave it in the cupboard most of the time and when I take it out it smells of mothballs. It has sweat marks on the armpits, but you can hardly see them.

It always looks like it's going to rain when people get married. I sit in my lounge chair facing the window and the view of the Brisbane River and listen to the races. I can see the clouds, over the top of my yellow racing guide, keeping the heat bottled in like it always does in summer.

George's daughter is getting married. I saw her grow into a woman. She is as lovely as her mother. She is probably getting everything ready, young Anne, in their house just around the corner. Her room is the one I used to sleep in, after a night with the boys when I was too drunk to ride or walk home, and she had to go and snuggle up with her parents. I can't count the times I woke up with a hangover and looked into that ugly mirror on the dresser, the one with little palm trees cut into the glass. She is probably looking into it right now.

I think of Anne and how old I am getting. My suit is old. It doesn't look like the ones advertised in magazines nowadays. My father wore his only suit to his wedding. For years I saw him in that suit in the wood and glass photograph frame at home, my mother wearing a huge lace gown. Father was smirking over her shoulder with his big smooth chin sticking out. He could've been a gangster, my father. They always wore those baggy suits. If he was, I never found out.

George's daughter will get her photograph taken today. Probably in one of those studios in the city that have canvas sheets that drop down, and you can make your choice if you want to stand in front of a forest or at the edge of a big lake.

George was miserable last night. He came around to my place, next to the brewery, with some cold bottles of beer. We sat and drank but he hardly spoke. He just watched the evening trains pass on the western line, across the road. The squares of sad yellow lights in every carriage like old teeth. He said that. The heads of passengers just cavities.

After a couple of beers we rode our motorcycles for a while. I followed George around the nearby suburbs. It amazed me after all these years how clean he kept his cycle. The lights at night bounced off it. We rode by the river, to the foothills near the city, past the bright yellow pub where all the students and rowers drank and back to my place.

He stayed fairly late and when the beer ran out we drank coffee. We sat and listened to the click of the brewery's new neon sign. Then he went home.

I can't imagine George in a suit, straightening his tie in the mirror and polishing his shoes. I'm not sure if he owns a suit. I have only ever seen him in overalls or leathers. It'll be a laugh seeing him all dolled up, sitting in those fancy cars with the ribbons all over them.

It's getting warm outside. I will have to iron my shirt soon. I hate the humidity because nothing moves in the heat. I see sparrows on the footpath and they are not moving. Maybe they are just the brown jacaranda flowers.

Anne is to be married in the brick church on the hill. I often wonder if the church bricks came from the same place as the brewery bricks next door. The church is on a ridge. From almost every street in George's suburb, over the tin roofs and trees, you can see the red church.

I drink a beer and listen to a couple of races before I wash up for the wedding. I even have a shave to go with my slicked back hair and dark suit. I know the suit will be hot. I will start to sweat as soon as I step into the trousers.

I have only met Anne's young man once. He is Catholic, George tells me. Makes no difference to me. He had short hair, blue eyes and shiny shoes when I met him.

I think I've only been to one wedding in my life. I go to church mostly for funerals. I have been to more funerals than weddings, I know that. There was Snake whose motorcycle was clipped by a car. And my father, but he was an old bastard near the end. I do remember a friend's wedding but it wasn't happy for me because there were flowers, just like Snake's flowers, and it was hard not to think of one without the other. The smell is always the same, too. A musty sort of smell.

I walk to the church because it wouldn't be right turning up at the grass car park next to the House of God on a black motorcycle. My mother is religious and hates motorcycles. She says it was because of the motorcycles that I never married. She says I have never grown up, and I have no answer to that.

Walking up the hill I remember when Anne first started going out with boys, to the city on Saturday nights or to Cloudland. One night George came round to my place and punched that hole in the door of my wardrobe. I knew it was because of the boys, and that his girl had become a young woman.

I arrive at the church gates and feel the sweat under my arms. The church smell is everywhere, even outside where the guests stand in groups. A lot of the women are wearing hats. One woman's hat has pretend fruit on the brim. The men all look the same in their suits with their shiny shoes. I look down at my shoes and there is a big scuff across the left toe. I walk to the side of the church and spit on the scuff but it doesn't go away. I think everyone is looking at my shoe when I join the guests and for the first time in years feel a bit self-conscious of the scar on my cheek.

I feel the sweat marks more in the cold church. It's almost painful under my arms. Inside people whisper. I sit by myself near the back and tuck my shoes under the purple kneeling cushions.

The bride's family and friends sit quietly on one side of the church. Across the aisle the groom's guests talk and laugh and shake hands, like they've already had a few drinks. Both sides glance at each other. It quietens down a bit when the priest arrives.

He wears a white smock and is very serious. His hair is shaved above the ears where there's a bit of grey stubble.

On top the hair is longer and strands fall across his forehead. He fills a big old goblet with wine and straightens a white cloth. It hangs over the edge of the marble altar. A red heart and gold cotton letters are stitched onto the front of the cloth. He opens a large Bible, puts in a yellow bookmark, and shuts it with a thud that echoes in the church.

I am watching the priest when Frieda arrives. She walks past me with her two older sisters and they whisper to some people before sitting at the front. Soon after the cars pull up in front of the church steps and the whole place is filled with the sound of their engines. People turn around to see the cars and the bride. I think they are looking at me so I also turn. I am really the first person to see Anne because I am right at the back and there is nobody between me and the front doors.

I quietly laugh to myself because it will be worth seeing George in a suit, without track mud or paint and oil all over him. Anne appears, beautiful in a long flowing dress. She almost glows in the light from the front entrance. A man in a black suit comes up beside her and I have to look twice because he is too big and tall to be George. His heels click on the concrete aisle.

As they pass my seat I see it is Frieda's brother Arthur. So he is to give George's daughter away. For a moment I feel like I'm at the wrong wedding and just a stranger in the big church. But when I think about it I'm not completely surprised. I should have realised. It was as plain as the hole in my wardrobe.

He's probably making something now, standing over his workbench under the house. He'd be smoking a cigarette and maybe cutting out the shapes of his hands for some leather gloves, or finishing off those fibreglass marker buoys the council asked him to make. He wouldn't be painting because it might rain. He'd be doing something. He wouldn't just sit around.

I feel a bit guilty, sitting in the church. I am after all George's friend from the motorcycle club. I'm the one who rides and drinks with him. I work on my motorcycle like he does. He swears and I swear. We both smoke. At least I am here at the wedding.

I don't understand everything the priest says. The ceremony is over and as the bride and groom turn to walk down the aisle an organist, somewhere behind all the flowers at the front, plays a final hymn. It's so loud it booms through the huge pipes. The bridal party and guests go down the aisle and I smell lavender and boot polish.

The priest has taken off his gown and stands on the front steps of the church. After a while he closes the green wooden doors and bolts them shut. I have been told the priest hates confetti. He hates it being thrown near the church because it blows under the front doors. It goes under the hymn book racks and gets stuck in the corners. Some has even been found in the baptism font. He folds his arms and looks like he's standing guard because if it gets under the doors it means he has to get up early on Sunday and clean it up before the morning service.

Handfuls of confetti are thrown over Anne and her husband John and I nearly break out laughing when waves of it are blown onto his arms and the doors. I see the priest watching it fall everywhere. He smiles but keeps looking at the confetti on the marble stairs.

A photographer has set up his black tripod and is holding up a flash. I look to the street and sort of expect to see George fly by on his motorcycle, looking through his old racing goggles at all the excitement. But I hardly see any traffic.

I feel like a smoke but I can't disappoint Frieda. I

can't puff away like George would. She's put up with a lot with him and his wheelbarrow full of butts under the house. He dumps them under bushes in the backyard.

The bridal party leaves in the white Fords. The cars are polished and I can smell the leather upholstery when the doors are opened and closed.

Frieda comes up to me. There's confetti stuck in her hair.

"Do you need a lift to the reception, Jack?" she says.

I remember I have no cycle and say yes. We leave for the function room in the city, on the banks of the river near the Storey Bridge. Arthur takes us in his Daimler. There are cigarette burns on the back seat where I sit between Frieda's two sisters, Gladys and May. Frieda sits in the front.

"It was lovely," Gladys says. "I'll never forget it as long as I live. Alf would have loved it."

Alf is her husband. He is not a well man, so George tells me. Used to be a sapphire digger and is still a communist. He subscribes to Russian magazines and hardly ever leaves the house.

"You'll have to get me some copies of the photographs, Frieda," May says.

The sisters look out the side windows. I sit with my hands between my knees. Arthur doesn't say anything on the way to the function room. He is a drinker, I am told. Works with a council road gang all day and drinks at night. His wife is always falling over and bruising herself, so Frieda says. She's a clumsy woman, that's all. He looks like a motion picture star behind the wheel with his clipped moustache and greased back hair. His cheeks are still pink from the barber's razor.

Frieda just looks through the windscreen.

I begin to sweat again in my suit, in between the sisters. Stale air builds up in the car. Occasionally my hair scuffs the roof, especially when we go over a bump. We approach the function room and May quickly winds down her window.

"I feel a bit sick," she says. "The heat."

Arthur drives with the skill of a chauffeur. He cruises to the edge of the footpath in front of a pink canvas awning.

"You get out and I'll find a park," Arthur says.

Guests peer into the car at us. May's face has turned white. I smell river mud. She holds a handkerchief to her mouth then puts her head out the window and pukes down the side of the car.

Gladys is silent. She turns her head away. I look through the windscreen and think of beer and cool air, and George. He wouldn't be home now. He'd be riding with a nice breeze on his face. He'd be riding for sure.

I hope there is a breeze on the walk home after the reception. It might even dry out my old suit, ready for the next time.

Mud and Ivory Elephants

I saw my mother's body one Sunday on the front page of a newspaper. I hadn't heard from her for five days because we had an argument over a pair of socks and there she was, just her calves and feet showing, half buried in river mud, in the newspaper. She only had one shoe on in the picture.

I had been to the pubs the night before with the boys from the garage where I worked. I got drunk and ended up sleeping on the beach down near the gymnasium. When I got home to my room at the boarding house the landlord was waiting for me with the newspaper and told me the police had been looking for me. He gave me a cup of coffee and I read about the woman found in the river.

Children had discovered her washed up on a bend, her body covered in silt. She still had a handbag over her shoulder, the newspaper said. And she wore an old ivory necklace of little carved roses and elephants. A policeman was quoted as saying she had not been positively identified, but I knew from the description of the necklace that it was my mother.

I still have the front page of the newspaper. It is

frayed along the folds. I took it with me to Australia because I thought it was important that my sister see it. I didn't know some of her friends had already sent it to her home at Sandgate. After a while it was not a sad story to read because it was not about our mother, but the body of a woman, written in clipped newspaper sentences. A woman without a name, in the cold river.

It was a silly argument, about the socks. Elaine was making a pair for me and so was my mother. Elaine was a quick knitter and she finished them in a couple of days. I was wearing them by the time my mother had finished the toe parts of her socks. Looking back I think my mother was in constant competition with Elaine, but she couldn't keep up. They argued, until I could not bring them together at all.

My mother kept telling me I was all she had after my sister left and married a pearl diver in Australia. She said Elaine was trying to steal me away from her. I told her that was a load of codswallop.

My mother had bad eyesight. They tried to tell me later that my mother just walked into the river. A doctor signed a paper that stated my mother was almost blind with cataracts. She could still knit though, I told them. She never had the lights on in the house much, and often she sat in the front room holding a handkerchief in the dark.

The newspaper said that there were no suspicious circumstances. I know that is their cute name for suicide. They never say "suicide" to save the family embarrassment and the strange looks from neighbours and shopkeepers. I didn't believe an argument over a pair of socks had caused it. It sounds bloody ridiculous but even now, whenever I put on a pair of socks, I think of my mother's death.

I have read lots of newspaper stories since then, about

ordinary men who kill someone over a woman, or a car, or money in old people's pockets, and I think what a fine line it is between being alive and dead.

The last time I saw Elaine was when I went to the river on that Sunday. She watched me from the bridge as I walked along the water's edge. I remember I looked up and she was there, leaning on the railing with her arms apart, watching me with my trousers rolled up to the knees. I wanted her to sod off. To let me poke through the reeds alone with a stick. I was looking for my mother's missing shoe. I felt that the river had stolen it from her. I know now it was a strange thing to do.

I went further around the bend and she moved along the bridge. The last I saw of her she was leaning out, holding onto the street lamp at the far end as I went out of view. I went into the reeds and found a path that children had made up into the village. I imagined she waited for me to come back from the river, muddied and damp.

I stayed in the gymnasium for a couple of days before I left to catch the ship. My friend, Dave, came with me. I'm not sure if Elaine followed us to the docks near the city. We stood on the ship's deck with hundreds of others. People down below threw streamers at us and long lines of stockings, the toes and waists tied together. The streamers tangled, and people cried on the ship and on the shore. I thought I saw Elaine with confetti in her hair.

I grabbed a red streamer and tried to find the stranger at the other end, but it disappeared into the crowd. The paper stretched and then flicked upwards as it broke, and down. Dave waved. As the ship moved away from the pier, men in small boats waited with sticks, ready to pluck the hundreds of broken streamers from the water.

*

The ivory necklace curled in the plastic bag next to the bundle of his mother's clothes and a moist shoe. The bag, a foggy sack. The identical cream flowers on the dress rotting, the mud still soft in cotton.

The bag was tied tightly at the top with a piece of twine. A tag was attached, the ink of her name smudged. George picked up the bag. A triangle of water formed in the corner, the mud thin and wispy like the long brown hair of a girl, diving.

He stood facing the counter in the police station, holding the bag up to the light. Drops streaked across plastic. The necklace was tangled. Tiny elephants dripped river water. The ivory rose petals between tails and trunks were clotted with mud. The stench from the dress took him momentarily back to the river. Into the bag of air and ivory. The necklace he bought his mother with his first pay packet.

He had seen the newspaper report about the drowned woman and rang his mother. When there was no answer he called the police and they asked him to come to the hospital. They said the woman had not been identified because she had been in the water for days. He thought of baths, white curves and swaying green water. It was his mother. He knew when he saw the necklace.

George gathered her clothes under his arm and held the plastic bag in his right hand. Elaine was there, her eyes red, swollen, sitting beneath the unshaven faces of wanted men on a noticeboard. He walked to his mother's empty house, blindly, as if he was swimming in the muddy river with his eyes open.

When George was young he swam with other boys in the river. They met at a secret clearing, not far from the bridge. The bank there was worn from wet feet with the fingerbones of roots on its surface. In summer the boys stripped off their school shirts and shorts, dropped the clothes in bundles or flung them onto the knife-points of reeds, and swam in their white undershorts. George preferred the excitement of the river to the local baths. He enjoyed the currents that buffetted his body, branches that brushed his legs in the murkiness and the dusk patterns of seeds and leaves on the surface. Later, at home, his mother would pick the seeds from his hair.

It was next to the river, squatting in a circle in a wet nest of reeds, that George and his friends learned about women. Magazines were smuggled into the circle. They peered at creamy limbs and silk as the evening cold came up through the mud. A mother's call from a kitchen window would send the boys skittering home, crushing reeds as they ran, the magazines left open. Naked women facing the sky.

In winter the boys lit small fires, fuelling them with exercise book pages and pencils. George loved the blue smoke and the warmth of the fire, so close to the river.

Years later he worked as a mechanic at Whitey's Garage and took his girlfriend Elaine down to the river bank for lunch. They sat in the park on the other side of the bridge. He looked through its stone arches to the patch of needle reeds and thought of strong liquor and the cigarettes he used to light from the fires. Elaine brought sandwiches for him and she ate fruit. He knew the conversation would lead to his mother.

"Is it going to be like this when we get married?" she said.

"Who the hell said we're getting married?" He rested on his left elbow on the grass and watched the pieces of straw and wood in the river ease past.

"Everyone expects us to," Elaine said.

79

"You mean your girlfriends at the gas company."

"Not just them, everyone."

"Everyone will have to wait," George said.

"Yes, until your mother is ready I suppose."

They had the same argument many times. George looked across to the trees, their corded roots clawing onto the bank. The roots emerging from the mud on the river bed.

"Maybe if your sister had stayed you wouldn't feel so guilty," Elaine said.

"I'm not guilty for anything," he said. "I'm her bloody son for Christ's sake. Stop pushing it."

They walked back to the centre of the village. She worked next to the jewellers and stopped there most times before going back to the office. George stood with her in front of the shop window and the dark reflection of his overalls was filled with arcing pearl necklaces, watches, velvet cases and gold claws gripping diamonds.

On Fridays he went to his mother's house for dinner. It was winter, cold and dark early. He rode under the balloon haze of streetlights to her house at the hill end of the village. She always turned on the downstairs light on Fridays and he coasted his motorcycle into the garage.

He took off his jacket and leather cap and walked up the backstairs in his steel-capped boots, the vibration from his weight deep in the house's foundations. He remembered the same shudder from when he was a boy. The clink of a tea cup, or an ornament, and the arrival of his father.

"Hello, mother."

She stood at the sink in the stark kitchen light, scrubbing a stain from the white china. She couldn't remove the shape of the flame where the cold water dripped onto the back of the sink. It wasn't as dark after her scrubbing, but it was still there.

"Have a nice day at work?" she said. "I can't get this stain off."

She kissed him on the cheek and he sat at his place at the table. Elbows on the tablecloth, pressing against a flight of food-specked geese. She went back to the scrubbing.

"You wouldn't think water could stain so bad," she said.

She went to the stove and stirred soup with a wooden spoon. George watched her concentrate on pouring the soup into a bowl, the steam across her powdered cheeks. The smell of tomato and talcum. For an instant, he saw the young woman in her face.

"What did the doctor say about your eyes?" he said.

"Not too good," she said. "They're getting worse. They don't seem any worse to me."

She poured a bowl of soup for herself and sat opposite George. She spilled some drops onto the tablecloth as she ate. Onto small wings.

She put her glasses on and took the fish from the oven.

"I'll get you some new glasses," he said.

"Don't want to waste your money. You've got to save now."

"What for?"

"For when you get married," she said.

"What has Elaine been saying to you?"

The smell of fish went right through the kitchen, its headless body arcing in the baking dish. The tail dry and stiff above simmering juice.

"I heard it down at the markets," she said. "I thought

you might have told me."

He saw the stars in a black sky outside the window. As he rode home after dinner he could still hear in his head the peck of cutlery on his mother's crazed china plate.

George's mother threw the socks into the fire. They burned quickly, the bone needles still embedded in the wool. It took a while for the bone to burn. He left after the argument and later imagined the needles, frail, with beads of ash at their ends, resting on the logs.

She knitted slowly because of her eyes, carefully locking the black fibre. Thick work socks for winter. Elaine made George a pair in a couple of nights. He wore them to dinner at his mother's house. They argued and he told her she was a silly old woman. It was the first fight they had had since his sister went to live on the other side of the world.

His mother threw her unfinished socks into the fire and he said he wouldn't come back until she made more sense. He stomped down the back stairs and rode away.

The boy told the police he saw a woman walk into the river. She was wearing a dress with flowers on it and carrying a handbag. Just walked into the river, as if it wasn't there. He didn't tell anyone for a couple of days because he was smoking cigarettes down in the reeds, and he was scared he'd get into trouble.

Police and volunteers went to the river and searched through the reeds on both banks. In the late afternoon, when the river rose slightly, people watching on the bridge could hear the sucking noises of men's boots being pulled from the mud. The searchers used torches, the blue beams cutting through the reeds. Thousands of strands, swelling at the waterline.

Someone yelled and there was a splash. The men rushed to the bend and pointed their torches at the woman's body. A statue in the silt. Blue light reflected off the mud. One of the men took a photograph and the flash turned everything white for a second. Then it was blue again.

George ran his thumb along the knobs of ivory, the smooth elephant shapes. Jagged rose petals. He felt the necklace through the plastic bag. He stood in his mother's kitchen, the tablecloth clean, the soup stains gone. He put the damp clothes and necklace on the table and went into the front room.

The sofa and chairs were just bulky shapes in the dark. Photographs on the wall stains in heavy wooden frames.

He went to her room, sat on the edge of the bed and switched on the bedside lamp. There, on the quilt, he saw a baby's pink cardigan. It smelled of mothballs. Its wool flat and dull, with knitted animals on each small pocket. The cardigan was neatly spread out, the arms outstretched as if in surprise. The buttons were so old they were cracked.

The tin gypsy wagon was next to the cardigan. George's childhood toy, with the smooth roof and square windows, painted red with gold lettering. The wheels loose, leaning inward.

He turned off the light and saw a glow from the village through the curtains. Spinning a wheel of the wagon, he thought he heard a young voice tangled in the squeak of tin.

Whalebone

My father was known as a Jack-of-all-trades in our suburb. Not a week passed when people didn't bring him dead irons, toasters with crumbs lodged between filaments, broken-down radios, plaster and wire lamps of naked women with bulbs in their upturned palms, cracked spectacles, even necklaces with the clasps worn through with age, or the constant turning of heads at parties. His mates towed their motorcycles on trailers to be fixed at our house, brought seized-up cameras, boots with worn heels, clogged taps from their kitchens and bathrooms, or scratched and dented pieces of cars.

He never took any money for the repairs. He lined up the objects on his bench downstairs, in the order of time they had been brought to him, and worked on them late at night. They may have lasted longer taken to repair shops in the city, to professional men in the field, but my father had the knack of making things work again, or making them look like new, if only for a short while. Those things he couldn't fix he handed back, defeated, and said he had done the best he could.

When something in our house broke down or fell apart, he had little time to fix it because of all the other jobs. When our iron suddenly cooled on my pleated skirt my mother put it at the head of the bench line to find days later that my father had pushed it to the back. He was working on a neighbour's cuckoo clock, and was having trouble getting the bird to come out of the little swing doors. He made his own parts out of pins, clips, wire, smoothed plaster over chipped ornaments and covered his work with paint.

The most unusual request came to him from Mrs Griller who lived a few doors down from our house. She was, my father called her, the mad sewing lady of Beck Street. When you walked past her house at night, you could see her head and shoulders, shadowy through the louvres on her closed-in verandah, bent over her old Singer, and hear the staccato bursts of the machine.

She made shirts and shorts for the summer babies of our street. Coats for boys who played in the gutter in front of her house. Blouses for church stalls. Acres of curtains. It was known, only amongst the women of Rosalie, that she was an underwear specialist and used fine materials brought by ship from England, taken home by her in double-wrapped brown paper parcels.

One day she came to our house and had tea. Over scones she asked George if he could, for a price of course, make her a tailor's dummy. If he could shape it to her exact proportions so she could make herself a winter wardrobe. It would be so much easier, she said, if she had such a dummy that she could shape the clothes on. It would be so much more professional.

My father was surprised but intrigued by the notion of Mrs Griller's torso. He told her he had never made such a thing. The closest he had come to that sort of work was the set of plaster bookends he made, the replica of his hands. It had not been easy, he told her, to make the hands. But he would like to try the dummy.

He told her to come over on Saturday afternoon and he would have the cloth and sticking plaster ready.

She left smiling, and when she had gone he whispered to us that considering the size of Mrs Griller he may have to buy several rolls of plaster. I laughed with my parents and couldn't wait for Saturday.

The torso was to be made in the kitchen. My father put a canvas sheet on the linoleum and laid out the cloth and sticky strips on the table. He hoped the sticky plaster would cling to the cloth, and the bumps of Mrs Griller, to create a mould.

She arrived wearing make-up and carrying a handbag as if she had an appointment at a beauty salon. My mother steered her into the kitchen. The curtains were drawn wide open for better light during the delicate operation.

"I'm not sure if this will work," George said, "but let's give it a try."

Mrs Griller stood on the canvas sheet. I saw her thick legs and bulging belly as I peered into the kitchen from the back landing.

"I'm afraid, Mrs Griller, that you will have to take your dress off," George said. She moved halfway off the sheet and looked to my mother.

"Must I do that?" she said. "Can't you make it without me having to do that?"

There was a moment's silence.

"I don't think so," he said. "The dress is too bulky. It will make the dummy bigger than you really are and I have to shape it as close as I can. Do you see?"

She tugged nervously at her dress.

"What do you want me to do then?"

"You'll need to undress to your underwear."

Mrs Griller had been a widow for years. Her skin was white. My mother took her into the bedroom and moments later she came out, her arms folded across her breasts. Her slip, with its elastic waist stretched tight, quivered at the bottom. She still had on her bright red shoes. Mrs Griller looked out the louvres for neighbours, or men mowing lawns.

"It shouldn't take long," George said. He wrapped her up in the cloth, starting at the neck and guiding it under her arms then down to her hips.

Mrs Griller, with her flabby arms stretched out to the sides, wore a magnificent whalebone corset. The type I had only seen on trips to town with my mother, in women's stores. A delicious caramel colour with windows of lace at the front and those swooping whalebone ribs sewn into the cloth, guiding the flesh upward and inward.

"When the sticking plaster takes to the cloth we'll be able to cut it off in one piece," George said.

Half an hour later we had tea with Mrs Griller sitting upright on a chair in the kitchen, stiffening in the breeze that came through the back door.

It took ages to firm and she sat there, motionless, as we busied around her, poking a shoulder-blade or collarbone. My mother read her snippets from the newspaper, played her songs on the radio and fanned her sweating face.

Finally George came up the back stairs with the giant tailor's scissors.

"Just keep still," he said. "It won't hurt a bit."

It was fortunate Mrs Griller had a sway back, creating a slight gap along her spine under the cloth and plaster. But it was a difficult cut. We heard things snap. Mrs Griller started breathing rapidly.

We were relieved when he finally broke through the plaster at the nape of her neck. Stretching open the torso, George stopped for a moment and turned to us.

"Can I take it off now?" Mrs Griller asked, still staring at the painting of ducks on the kitchen wall.

We looked into the opening and saw, with horror, that George had cut clean through her corset and bra strap as well. The strips of whalebone poked out of the limp elastic. She had big freckles on her back.

Before we could say anything Mrs Griller, the sweat running down her face, pulled off the mould.

Mrs Carten from across the road said at church on Sunday that she too had heard the scream from our house and thought murder, finally, had come to our quiet suburb.

Mrs Griller avoided my father after that Saturday in the kitchen. If she saw him in the local shop she hid behind shelves. She watched him walk up the street through gaps in her curtains. He had been, after all, the only man since her husband to have seen her partially naked.

She never got her tailor's dummy. She put on some of my mother's underwear that day and walked briskly back to her house. She didn't sew for weeks.

My father kept the failed torso. He showed it to his mates and was, I believe, quietly smug that he at least had the exact, if not hollow, shape of a woman's breasts set in plaster and cloth.

It did not go to waste. For years it rested in the small rectangular garden patch under the back stairs, and in its ample breast cups he grew the prettiest maidenhair I have ever seen.

Museum:
from George's Notebook

Why is it when something dies you think you can still see it, that it's still around, not long after. It was the same with Bunty my bulldog. She died but I thought I could see her after, on the back landing or under the poinciana, but it just turned out to be the rubbish bin or a pile of raked grass. Even when my mother died I thought it was her standing near the door but it was just her old coatstand. If I looked into the dark long enough I could make shapes out of it and bring her back for a moment. Little things kept reminding me of her like her apron or all those glass bowls and the perfume bottle she kept on her dresser. They were really only junk when she was alive but my sister has them now, wrapped in pink tissue paper in a box.

Whenever I have to tell people about what happened to my mother it sounds stupid. You never think that your mother will drown. After a while you begin to think it never happened that way and you're talking about somebody else. I thought she'd die in a home or in a hospital like everyone else. I have to say she just walked into a river when I'm not even sure if it was an accident. By the look on people's faces I know they're wondering too. She must have felt the water in her shoes. She had bad eyesight, but to keep walking? How can I tell them she still held onto her handbag? I ask myself a thousand times who's to blame.

I don't even know why I keep my mother's clothes and her bag. The dress and underwear are still stiff with mud because I have never washed them. Sometimes I squeeze the black bag I keep them in to feel how hard the clothes are. I still have her glasses in their leather case. I have taken them out a few times and tried to blame them for not being strong enough for my mother's eyes. That's how bloody mad you get.

I've tried to clean the big ivory necklace but I can't get the mud out. It's in all the crevices of the roses and the elephants. It would take ages to pick out the mud. Even if I took it to a proper jeweller and got him to clean it, he would ask questions too and I'd have to go through the whole story again. The more I tell it the more I don't believe it. I've thought about throwing everything away and making up a story that she had a heart attack or just died in her sleep and telling it so often that I believed it. I don't think it will ever work that way. I think of her and still love her but the bitch drowned and left me wondering. Something I can never keep a secret, especially from myself.

*

I went to the old house for the first time to pick up Frieda to go to the pictures. Someone left a shovel on the grass out the front and weeds had grown around it. I didn't think anyone was at home at first because all the windows were shut. It was a shabby green house and the paint was peeling off.

I knocked on the door and Frieda opened it. She looked lovely and younger than the last time I saw her, but Jesus the house stank of cooked meals, a sort of sweet smell. It was so dark inside I could just see the parents across the room, sitting next to a big black piano. The father was asleep on the couch and he made little fish noises through his open mouth. The mother was in a chair next to the couch, knitting.

When Frieda closed the door it was quiet and I didn't know what to say. The mother's knitting needles clicked like the sound of my old man's teeth when he ate dinner. She was a bloody big woman. You could see straight away she wore the pants in the house. The poor little bastard was still asleep on the couch. Her face looked yellow in the dim room, her mouth a slit and a ball of hair on the back of her head.

Frieda introduces me and the woman doesn't even get up or stop knitting, just nods her head. I probably imagined it but the knitting seemed to get faster and faster. The first thing she says to me is she doesn't like young men on motorcycles roaring up to her house and would I leave the noisy thing down the street so she didn't have to set eyes on it and the neighbours would have no cause to complain. Lovely bloody welcome I thought. The woman's mad. What else can I say but okay?

I stand there like an idiot and try not to look at her. No wonder Frieda likes getting out on my cycle in the fresh air. The father wakes up and doesn't seem to know where he is because it's so dark. He's a thin man with strands of hair across his balding head. He shakes my hand and creeps out to the kitchen. I feel sorry for the poor bastard.

Anyway, I'm about to leave the house and I've forgotten I dumped my leather head-piece and gloves on the mother's good dining room table. Before I know it she's

91

grabbed them and walked out onto the front landing. She waited until Frieda and I followed her and then tossed them over the edge, smiling as they floated down to the grass. Then she went back inside.

Even as Frieda and I ride through Rosalie on the way to the Plaza the smell of the house is still with me, in my shirt and hair. It lingers, as they say, like the smell of death in an old man's pyjamas.

*

It scared me at first but now I am fascinated by the streams of blood that flow down the white toilet bowl into the water. I think about it in bed at night or when I'm working. It has been happening for months now.

I make sure the wooden lock on the bathroom door is flicked across and I urinate and watch. I never used to give the little room on the back verandah a second thought. I never even used to shut the door once. But suddenly I know the room's every detail. The paint that has been worn away around the handle. The bottle of disinfectant as brown as whisky. The paper roll on the wire holder I made out of a coat hanger. The ripples in the fibro walls. The small window with the foggy louvres. Not to mention the calendar I never hated up until now. It has an ugly brown map of the world on it, drawn centuries ago by an explorer or so the inscription says. The names and lines on the map are almost too faint to read, and I can't make out which continent is which. It's the type of calendar you can only rip the months off so I can't get a new picture unless I get rid of the whole bloody year.

I know what the blood means and Frieda would know if I told her. I just have to be a bit more careful. I've even made a game out of the blood and try to make out pictures in the lines, like the profile of a face or a animal, or even a bit of coastline I'm familiar with. It has never been scrubbed better in its life, that bloody toilet bowl. I have to do it to get rid of the blood. I'm pretty lucky the toilet brush is pink, or somehow I'd have to clean it as well.

*

Frieda has put a framed picture of me on the cupboard I made her, in the kitchen. She insisted I have a proper photograph taken in the studio in Queen Street. It makes me wonder if she knows about my illness. She has plenty of photographs of me, on cycles, with trucks I have painted, at a picnic with Anne in my arms. The only other time I had been in a photograph studio was when I was a child. I don't remember going there but I still have the picture. I am sitting on a blanket in front of a pot plant which sprouts up behind my head. The name of the photographer is written in the corner, just under my right heel.

I eat dinner at the kitchen table and look at the framed photograph beside the fish tank. My hair is white and my neck looks so thin. Any fool could tell I'm getting old too quickly. My muscles are just wasting away. My skin looks mottled in the mirror but it's pink in the photograph. The photographer must have painted me over with a little brush in the back of the studio. He probably guessed I was sick and thought the thick paint might save me or make me live a little longer, then sealed me under the glass so my face wouldn't crack or bend.

I should have smiled in the picture. It's funny but sitting under those hot lights with Frieda at the back in the dark I had a feeling it wasn't for fun but for family history. A final portrait of me.

I know it will sit there on the shelf when I'm dead. It has no life in it now because I'm still here, sitting at the kitchen table. When I go it'll be the same picture but it'll come to life. It'll be one of those things that my wife will keep and give to my daughter later on.

Even that stupid fish and all the plants and pebbles in the tank will disappear. Maybe someone will repaint the cupboard like I should have done ages ago. But I'll still be there in the frame proud as punch. All that, and the picture only cost me a lousy quid.

*

After all these years it's just the blue paper and the handwriting that I love now. The words are shaped so nicely in big loops. Elaine must have spent hours and hours writing to me although she doesn't live that far away. I feel like a bastard sometimes because I'm happy she has no one. She even said to me in one of her letters that I wanted to own everyone I ever met and liked.

I could have gone to see her in the house somewhere across the bay near my sister's place. Frieda doesn't know but I've headed off to see her and ridden quite a way before turning back just after the bridge. There was a shoulder of dirt there where I always used to turn and come home. It was always smooth because cars would whiz past and the air would flatten out over the tracks of my motorcycle.

If the council had ever decided to bitumen it I might have been forced to ride on and go the whole way. But they didn't.

Frieda has said the same thing to me, that I can't let

people go. She calls me the great collector. I should have worked in a museum, she says. I could walk all day through the rows of cabinets and look at all the shells, dead insects, gadgets, photographs, war relics, and dust those dummies that stand in a line behind the red ropes and are meant to show man's evolution since the ape.

I guess I do collect some things but not to build up a picture of the past or bring it back or even be close to it. I don't even want to touch it, although Frieda doesn't believe me. I just like to have solid things around me to keep me going. My museum is a different museum, I think. One that moves around, backwards and forwards. And unlike the others it's one that you don't belong to when you're dead.

*

Sometimes the smell of the mud is stronger than the leather. In summer I can smell the mud as the breeze cuts up Herschel Street and around the corner past my shoe repair shop in George Street.

It is too small in here for me. The shop is just a wedge of space. It's wide at the front and narrow at the back, with just enough room for a sink.

My brother-in-law calls it a good business venture. I sit behind a bench all day with a mound of leather scraps, hammers and sharp blue tacks. I have glue, and shelves to put the shoes on when I've finished working on them. I put yellow tickets on the heels so people can get back the right shoes.

I get all kinds of shoes. Army boots that may have seen action in Europe, or maybe never even left the country. I don't know. I get women's shoes with rips or snapped heels. Maybe the heel was broken over a man's head in an argument, or against a street gutter. I never know unless people tell me the story of their shoes.

Some shoes have mud on the outside or sand inside and they tell their own story. Some with bits of grass stuck to the sides that I know must have fallen apart that day, in the early morning on the way to work with the dew still moist in the leather.

Lots of people expect me to make new shoes out of their old ones. They look a little disappointed when I fix the shoes and they are still dull or the same. I can't perform miracles with a ball-headed hammer and a box of tacks. And some of the shoes smell. I know the smell of the person from the shoes. That's why it's nice to smell mud and mangroves from the Brisbane River for a change.

I have discovered there is no money in feet. They are at the forgotten end of the body, feet. Most of them are covered in knobs and lumps with the bone stretching the leather and sweat staining the lining. But I like the way the brand names are worn through on the soles and you can tell the type of person by the way the scuff marks streak back. Whether the person is fat or thin, puts more weight on the left or right foot or has a special walk. It's interesting but too small here for me. All I have all day is rows of shoes to work on. If the people stayed and talked for a while it would be all right, but they just leave behind their shoes.

*

I go to see Dorothy up at the hospital every month. She went funny after she had the kid. Cec had to bring up the boy by himself all those years.

The hospital is on a hill and the lawn goes right down

to a wire fence. Frieda and I sit with her on the lawn and I can't stop thinking that she was a normal woman before the kid. Now she spends her whole time in a nightdress.

We can see the river from where we usually sit. It's not as wide as down near the city, and I've heard people have canoed all the way up to the bridge near the hospital. What Dorothy really loves is the train. She can only hear it from the lawn, and I suppose the window of her bedroom, but when it passes she looks out into the trees.

It's the only thing she really responds to except for me. She looks at me when I talk. I am the only person she does that to, Frieda says. Not to any of the doctors, nurses or warders when they yell at her and take her back to her room. Not even Cec. She only listens to me.

*

There was no funeral for my son. I remember it was just a small service in the chapel at the back of the hospital. The chapel wasn't even as big as the waiting room for the fathers and relatives. It had a wooden cross on the wall and chairs facing the cross.

They had to telephone for a priest. It didn't take long for him to arrive and then it was just me and the matron and the priest. A couple of my best mates waited outside because they were still in their overalls. They took their hats off though because they had them in their hands when I came out.

The people at the hospital didn't let me see Frieda for what seemed like a long time. The whole thing was not real for me because I expected the child for so long and then there was nothing to hold or see in the cribs with the other babies. Everyone said to have some time off work but I didn't want to.

I think of my son and how he would have been a man now. He could've ridden with me or raced with my mate's sons. I only have a piece of paper typed on an old machine because some of the letters are crooked. It has his name on it. They asked me what we were going to call him and they put his name on the paper. I can take it out and read it any time I want. Jim Baker — stillborn.

*

It's beautiful when the faces start coming through the paper. I love to move the paper from side to side in the chemicals in the sink and watch the pictures appear. If it's just a shot of a face the nose never comes out first, as you would expect because it sticks out from the face in real life. Usually the skull line comes first with the babies, and the outline of the hair with men and women. Then there's the neck or the patterns of a shirt.

The best part is when the pictures start to get richer, the eyes begin to open and the lips look like a line of pencil. I know the difference in the shapes of my twin grandchildren's heads and the angles at which their ears poke out. Their eyes are two different shades of grey. I can almost see what they are going to look like when they get older, the way the jaws will go and how the noses will shape.

I have no choice really. I look for their future through the developing chemicals in my old white sink in the darkroom.

*

My sister has tried everything. It upsets me to see her like this. She has brought in the Christian Scientists. They came all the way from Brisbane in a bus. I don't know how they carried the books.

The Roman Catholic priest came in through the back door like he did it every day of the week and talked to me while he drank coffee. They won't let me have coffee any more, even though I've snuck a couple of cups in the morning before everyone was awake, so I dislike him for his steaming cup that he sips in front of me. He said men like me often turn to God in their hour of need. I think they were the words he used. He said there was no sin in that. I shouldn't have laughed because he was older than me and was trying to do the right thing.

Even the local psychic came to see me. She said she saw blue skies ahead and that I would get better in no time. I had a long lifeline across my palm, she said. I asked her to come closer when she spoke, and she did. Only because I liked the smell of her, oatmeal soap I think it was, and could see my face in the tiny mirrors in her earrings.

How many times do I have to tell them I didn't come to the bay to die, but for the smell of the sea?

*

I've found a hole under the chair where I hide the cigarettes. Good old Jack brought them for me, although I'm not supposed to have them. I get up before everyone else and in the mornings they ask me where the smell is coming from. Sometimes I say I burned the toast, or that the neighbours were burning rubbish. Other times I say what smell? I don't smell a bloody thing. You've all gone mad, I say. What a lark.

Thieves

They stole everything when my grandfather died. Cleared his bench of tools. Carted away boxes of motor-cycle trophies, paint tins and his photographic equipment from the darkroom. His truck was driven away.

After the funeral my grandmother stayed with her sister in Sydney. When she came back there was nothing left of George. Only a ball-headed hammer, a carpenter's pencil and some clothes. They were only spared because they were in a cupboard upstairs, inside the locked house.

I have always looked upon my relatives as thieves. My great-uncle, who left George's expensive photograph printer on a pawn shop shelf in Fortitude Valley. His wife who cut up raw sheets of leather and slid them on top of her claw-footed piano. A man known to my mother as Uncle Frank, although he wasn't a real uncle, who took his best friend's truck and used it for years to carry planks and nails across the city before it broke down and the tyres went flat, in his backyard near the bay. All thieves.

There is an urgency to tidy and clean after death. The relatives had two weeks before Frieda came back from

100

Balmain. In that time pieces of George were spread across Brisbane. In workshops and drawers under houses. Beneath canvas canopies in backyards. In the corners of toolsheds, or on mantelpieces.

I try to imagine these people, the fragrance of funeral flowers still in memory. The tone of my grandfather's voice able to be clearly remembered. All of them instantly able to recall his favourite phrases, his infectious laugh. His fingerprints smudged on steel and wood under the house. And the people moving in, cautiously at first, carrying warm objects at dusk into cars and trucks and living rooms. Bent elbows as they made their way home.

Shortly before his death George sold his motorcycle to a well-known collector. He made sure the buyer was genuine and would look after the machine. It caused arguments, the missing Matchless, between his club friends who didn't know of the sale. They came around looking for Satan and accused each other of taking it. They squabbled and shoved shoulders. I don't know if it was intentional that George sold the motorcycle before he died and left his friends with just its oil stain on the concrete.

*

George died in a leather chair in his sister's house by the bay. He was taken back to Brisbane in a white ambulance and cremated on the outskirts of the city, in a building that looked like an Indian temple. A mason symbol was forged in steel above his name on a plaque. His ashes were put in a small black box and pushed into a cavity in a brick wall, in the crematorium gardens.

Dozens of people attended the ceremony. George's friend, Jack, gave a short speech. Someone placed

George's motorcycle boots on the coffin, the worn straps and buckles rising from the flowers, the toes facing the congregation. His friends from the club stood at the back of the chapel against the wall. Their leathers creaked.

A few of them returned week after week to look at the plaque in the wall. Thought they could hear his laughter and the clink of beer bottles at the wall of ashes. Once, a friend abused the crematorium gardener for not watering the rose bushes beneath George's plaque. He grabbed a watering can and doused the bushes himself. After a while there were less visits to the crematorium. The gardener pinned a note to the back of the door of his shed, "George Baker Row C 17", and spent more time caring for the roses, afraid the angry man would return. Flowers bloomed, but the man never came back.

"Go and see May and we'll take care of everything here for you," Frieda's brother Arthur told her. The family ate sandwiches after the funeral. The food was prepared hours before the ceremony, put under tea towels of painted birds and bagpipe players, on a kitchen table. The men drank beer although it was only late morning. George would have liked it that way, they said.

"It'll be like a holiday," Arthur said. "You've never had a real holiday." She could sit by the harbour. Catch a ferry to Manly and walk through the Corso. She could go to the zoo.

They took Frieda to South Brisbane station. Carried her luggage. She saw them through the carriage window as the train began to move. They waved vigorously. The women shook white handkerchiefs. They disappeared, and the bunch of flowers she held rocked with the rhythm of the train.

May lived in a brick block of flats at Balmain. She lived on the ground floor and her unit faced a small park. Rusted swings in thick grass. She had a small concrete patio where she kept rows of pot plants. The front doormat said *Welcome*. The door had a frosted glass piece in its centre and when visitors dropped by you could see them, outside, their heads and shoulders blurred.

May loved ornaments and souvenirs. A cheap oil of the Sydney Harbour Bridge hung on the wall in the loungeroom. Models of ferries sailed on top of the piano. Tea towels over the stove handle showed a moist, warped Circular Quay.

"I tried to make it to the funeral, Frieda, but I couldn't get anyone to mind the cat," May said.

She made tea and they sat at the kitchen table. For Frieda, it was almost like being at home in Brisbane. The tea pot. The round currant buns on a plate. But the light was different. An afternoon sun was not as clear as at home. It was grainy, between houses and above roofs. Strange, the old copper green in the crevices of the bridge and lights on the surface of the harbour.

At night, May played the piano. Old-fashioned lace notes that reminded Frieda of when the three sisters had lived together as children and were all learning how to play the piano. When they fought to get on the stool. The creak of pages in the sitting room, the black dots and lines and the sheets of music in the piano seat. Practising for their mother who sat in the chair by the window, her head back and her eyes closed, as if absorbing the notes. The daughters who were not playing standing beside the piano, watching her face, looking for the slightest hand movements, eager to play.

She thought of her father who loved to hear the music. A short, wiry man who worked downstairs all day, his legs crossed, on top of a wooden table. Surrounded by rolls and scraps of material, holding the large black scissors that shaped a thousand suits. They called him their little Chinese tailor.

After dinner the girls would go into the backyard, the corners thick with weeds. Behind the fence was the railway line. May, the eldest, used to scare her sisters by threatening to throw them under the wheels of an evening train. Toss them right over the choko vines.

May had another cup of tea when she finished playing the piano. The model ferries had moved slightly, pushed by waves of heavy bass. May had strong hands.

Frieda began to miss her friends, her house. The familiar groan of the tin roof before an afternoon storm. Steam off the road and water rushing down gutters, eddying in the driveways. The coolness under the house. Cold kitchen lino.

She sat on May's patio at dusk and watched the children in the park. The same children came every afternoon. They crawled over swing limbs until it was dark and she could not see the swings, only the bright clothes of the children twisting and turning in the air. The children giggled and whispered, words lost in the grass, until the streetlights flickered on and they ran home.

"I have to get back to see my grandchildren," Frieda said one night, after the piano-playing. Strings vibrating from the final chord.

"Good," May said. "I'm just about out of tea anyway."

Frieda's older brother, Henry, and his wife were the first to look around the house. They lived across the road and could see the fibro house from their bedroom window. He had sat on his front steps every afternoon since Frieda had gone and looked over at the locked house. One evening, when the neighbours were eating dinner, the smell of vegetables and fat in the street, they went to the house. They inspected George's workbench and shelves in the dark. Squinted into the truck and the darkroom.

The next evening they brought cardboard boxes. One each. The light from nearby kitchens and living rooms gave George's belongings an odd glow. They took chisels and paint brushes. Lifted leather boots from the shadows. Henry's wife was obsessed with spoons. She had hundreds, from souvenir shops around the world, at home. She took all the teaspoons from the shelves and George's coffee thermos, its tartan pattern streaked with old coffee lines.

No one saw them walking back across the road that night hugging the full boxes. It would not have mattered if they had been seen. They were relatives of the man who had died. People do odd things in mourning.

Days later, George's motorcycle club mates pulled up outside the house in a utility. They wanted to see Frieda about the trophies. Dozens of tin trophies that George had won over the years. Tarnished lids and handles. On the top, tiny motorcycles or helmets. The club would like to have them in its glass trophy cabinet in memory of George, the daredevil rider who painted the face of Satan on the fuel tank of his Matchless. Who was the first man in Brisbane to make fibreglass motorcycle helmets, or "skid-lids". They found some trophies under his work bench.

They also found new tins of paint. George would have wanted that; a new coat of paint on the clubhouse. And the boot buckles and straps could be used. It was heavy, George's industrial sewing machine. The rear tyres of

105

the utility bulged under its weight. It all fitted neatly in the back.

Frank came. He remembered that George had promised him the truck, one night at a hotel. George had said, "Frank, if anything happens to me the truck is yours, I want you to have it." He knew where George kept the keys, on the rusted nail in the beam above the bench. He lifted the keys off the nail and left the keyring in a pot plant on the shelf.

It took a while to start the truck. It groaned in the space under the house. The neighbours saw him back the truck out of the yard and went about their business. Across the road, Henry leaned on the sill of his bedroom window. Frank drove past, and they waved to each other.

Frieda's younger brother, Arthur, mowed her grass while she was away. He sweated over the hand mower for hours, tore out weeds from around stumps and the poinciana tree, and filled the incinerator with clippings. Flowers shook under hose water. He sat on a chair under the house when he had finished and wondered what had happened to the truck. The drip tray was still there, blotched with oil.

He put the rake back in the darkroom, and ran his hands over the photograph printer. It was an awkward green metal object. He didn't know how it worked. It looked expensive, he thought. The powerful light buried in its head. George once told him it was a machine that pulled people, mountains, trees, fast cycles and oceans from paper.

The pawnbroker liked the machine so much he put it in his front window, facing the street, behind the security bars and glass. He removed the tray of watches, most of them wound down, so the printer could have pride of place. Near its heavy base were dead flies in dust.

"You sure it works?" he asked Arthur. "I seen the light on but does the thing work?"

"You won't get another like it," Arthur said. "It came all the way from England. It was in a magazine."

"It was in a magazine?" the pawnbroker said, delicately turning a black knob.

"In a magazine," Arthur nodded.

The pawnbroker raised his eyebrows and looked at the printer. He changed the price he had put on a tag and the two men shook hands. Arthur had whisky in the cupboard for a week after that.

George's sister Nell came to Brisbane on a bus to clean the house for Frieda before she came back home. She had the spare key, polished the oak dining table and pulled dead leaves off plants. She put the pot of maidenhair in the kitchen sink and left the tap dripping onto it. She only just made the bus back to Sandgate, putting the two full string bags on the seat beside her.

They didn't touch the leather chair. Frieda wanted it after George died and friends brought it to her house after the funeral. They left it downstairs, under the grey gas meter, its dials motionless. Frieda told them it would be safe there.

Nell was glad to get rid of it. It was an old chair, the stuffing yellow and compressed by hundreds of bodies. Settled into the shapes of thighs and spines. A clot of straw often warmed by distant blood. The wooden armrests were worn smooth and blotched with muddy varnish.

A cat discovered the chair while Frieda was away. It savoured the chair's smell and warmth. The danger in the leather. A looming animal much larger than the cat. It slept on the chair at night, drunk on leaking gas.

Frieda arrived home in the late afternoon. She walked from the station. She checked her black tin letterbox on the post and stood in the front yard with bags in each hand. She trembled slightly, the clatter of train still with her.

She could see the wooden stumps of the house, thick and grained, and the railway tracks that had been used as beams to hold up the structure. Slipped under when it was lifted, decades ago. She could see straight through under the house, the copper, the peg basket, pipes, the floodwater drain and into the backyard. She could see the roots of the poinciana tree, twisted arms in the dark grass. She had never been able to see through to the backyard before. Not with George's motorcycle, his truck, giant plywood signs, canvas, metal drums and stacked coffee tins always there.

She put down the bags and went under the house. Stood on the concrete slab and looked over the bench, the shelves. She couldn't remember what had once been there. What had gone and created the open spaces. The feel of quiet shoes, flashing hands. Human tracks that she couldn't see on the lawn and concrete.

She found a pale nest of cat hairs on the seat of the leather chair. She turned the gas on.

Frieda never found out where everything disappeared to. Months after her return, letters and notes of explanation turned up in her letterbox. Relatives asked her to lunch and casually mentioned tools, or pieces of leather they had seen and thought she would have thrown away anyway. Others didn't say anything at all and when she asked about George's things, they said George had given them the spray-painting gun, or sheets of wood, a long time before he passed away.

Downstairs, the breeze pushed over concrete, nail heads in the floorboards and through to the backyard. Dead poinsettia leaves scratched across the concrete. Before, when George was alive, the breeze swirled over the mudguards of the truck. Along the razor edges of tools. Shuffled mounds of shavings. Now she could almost feel the body of air under the house, flowing through like the creek that, centuries ago, had passed where the house was to be built and still ran, deep in soil, around roots and the buried rubbish of unknown people.

It was solid under the house, with George. She sat on the edge of the couch watching television. Uneasy, as if the house was suspended. Not part of the earth, but tied down to it.

*

I have heard that men and women try to preserve the memory of the dead. They leave deathbeds unmade for years, the shape of the body still visible on white sheets. They keep strands of hair in brushes, or trim it and put it in envelopes. Suits, frocks, hats, belts, stockings and shoes are locked in cupboards. I have even heard of entire bedrooms being sealed. Never opened until new people move in, or the house is destroyed by fire, bulldozers.

My grandmother still had some of George's clothes. Not all of them. She gave a lot away to second-hand stores. They were hung on racks, next to other old clothes, and taken away by strangers.

She gave me a pair of his overalls when I was older. I have them, protected from insects, in a plastic bag. They have oil spots on them, like continents on a map, but blurred through the plastic as if just under the surface of water.

She said most of his other things were taken away. Maybe some of them ended up in suitcases in the country, or in cities down south. Stored in drawers and cupboards thousands of miles away.

She recently visited Aunt Nell and noticed one of George's plaster figures in a cabinet. He made little sculptures of motorcycles and riders. Tiny men wearing helmets and goggles. My grandmother asked Nell about the motorcycle in the cabinet and Nell said she had had it for years. There was dust on the rider's helmet, between the goggle straps. For years, she said, as if it had always been hers.

The motorcycle was hers now, my grandmother told me later. She had no feeling of ownership any more. As if George had faded from it, and now it was Nell's. As if its origins had been forgotten, or become uncertain, and now the motorcycle was someone else's, resting on the mirrored shelf of the cabinet.

Envelopes

It was the mice that finally brought us together. I thought that was rather funny after living with this woman for fifty years. I didn't really live with her, but she was always somewhere in the house, before and after George died. It might have been a photograph of her hidden in the back of his workbench drawer. Bits of her hair in envelopes, or those bundles of scented letters.

I kept Elaine's photographs and letters to George in two brown paper bags. When I was tidying up after he died I collected them together, tied the bags with string and put them in the cupboard under the green gas cooker. For years after reminders of her kept appearing. A tangled red hair ribbon in a suitcase, an inscription in a book, her name engraved near the hinge of one of his old cigarette cases.

It was annoying at first but it means nothing now. We are old women. We wear the same types of stockings I'm sure, rolled just above the knee where the skin is loose. We wear cardigans and carry handkerchiefs with tiny cotton violets stitched into the corners. Our brushes are knotted with grey hair.

I had almost forgotten about the letters when the mice

came. The trouble began in my black piano. It drifted out of tune, and the piano man told me he found the skeleton of a mouse caught up in the bass strings. I dropped chemical cubes into the piano and shut the lid.

Soon after, the mice moved into the kitchen. There were so many of them I could hear them scratching when I boiled the kettle, or cooked my Sunday roast. My friends at the church told me to use traps. Not the small ones, because they were not strong enough, but large traps designed for rats, triggered by the slightest movement. The big traps broke their necks, or even their backs, depending on the courage of the rat, they said. I had seen these traps in supermarkets and didn't like the look of them, all wire and wood in cardboard bins.

The pest man arrived. He wore a cap with a green cotton cockroach stitched onto its peak. He carried a scratched cylinder with a hose coiling from its top. At the end of the hose was a long, thin steel rod.

"Where's your problem, lady?" he said.

He got on his knees and put his head into the cupboard under the cooker. He still wore his cap. He shone a small black torch inside the cupboard.

"Lots of 'em. You got a nest here." He said the paper bags may have brought the mice and caused them to nest in the warmth under the cooker.

I took everything from the kitchen cupboards and he sprayed. He said he would come back later in the week to remove the bodies. It seemed odd to call them bodies but I suppose it was his job and important to him.

The grocery bags of letters had been damaged by the mice. There were holes in the corners and string had been gnawed. They had eaten through the ankle of the green ink woman on the side of one bag and the wheel of the trolley she was pushing on the other. Some of the letters had also been chewed — the "Street" or "Brisbane" of addresses and the head of a Royal on stamps, all swallowed.

I didn't want to keep the bags any longer. I didn't feel safe with them in the house, as if they produced the mice themselves. I put both bundles of letters into a large plastic garbage bag. The day after the pest man cleaned the cupboards I caught the bus to Sandgate. Elaine had lived in the area since my marriage to George, all those years ago.

I held the bag of letters in my arms and as the bus jolted I could feel the sharp-edged envelopes and photographs against my forearms. Days later, as I knew, my arms would be bruised a blue as pale as the shade of air mail paper.

*

I travelled to Sandgate often as a child. It was popular then and far enough from Brisbane to make it an adventure. I remember going on the weekends with the family in my father's spoke-wheeled car, arriving at the beach and seeing people in black or striped bathing costumes. Only ladies' ankles and knees were allowed to show back then.

In the early evening my parents would go to dance in the big blue hotel by the bay. My brothers and sisters and I would curl up in the car that faced the beach, in a row with lots of other cars, and fall asleep as the bass notes plodded out from the ballroom. When we woke up we were home.

I don't like the place much any more, with its seafood shops and windows of boiled crabs, prawns and bugs, all in plastic buckets of ice. And I hate seeing those poor lobsters in the aquariums in restaurants, the points of their legs barely touching the coloured stones. The worst thing is seeing the napkins and knives and forks on tables through the murky water.

From the bus window I can see the old pier and its rotting stumps rising from the water. Beside it is a steel and concrete jetty with red poles and railings. And the old bathing pavilion is still there. I used to think it was a lovely building but now it's just an ugly shell of archways and fake columns. Young people have spray-painted obscenities on its walls, pictures of naked women and what look like lizards.

Sometimes I can still feel the old days at Sandgate. There are flashes of them, in the felt of an old man's hat, the way the bitumen roads crumble at the edges or beer smells from hotel windows. I'm glad in a way that the house where George died has gone because if I saw it again the memories would come back too easily. It's easier to cope if there's a bit of distance.

The bag of letters slumps on the seat beside me. During the trip it shifts with the sway of the bus and bulges over the seat edge. I straighten it but it slides towards me, the dozens of envelopes moving. I'll be glad to get rid of this bag. The heavy plastic makes my arm sweat.

We are nearing the street. I have never been to this part of Sandgate but I know the area. The street in black ink. The beach a yellow slab. It's green where the beach overlaps the blue bay. The street names are written in red. I have studied the area in the street directory and looked down upon the woman and her street, the roof of her house somewhere in the whiteness between the black lines.

I know Elaine will be home. Old women only go out for special reasons, to take fruit to friends in hospital or to go to church. I used to go to the supermarket every week for food but now I have it delivered. A young man in running shoes brings the groceries in cardboard boxes which I burn in the backyard when I've put everything in the cupboards. That's how the neighbours know when I get food. Your world gets smaller when you're old. It closes in.

I guess that's why I wanted to return the letters. What was written so long ago really means nothing. They are just envelopes. A bag of loose ends, all unsealed with their blue flaps and dull strips of glue.

And I wanted to meet the woman who had fascinated my husband. The woman who nearly married him, followed him and wrote to him for years, lived a dozen streets from where he died, and spent all her life alone.

*

For a long time after George's funeral I thought she had been to our house. When I came back from my sister's in Sydney and everything of his had been taken away, I imagined her there.

She may have been across the street at night, standing on the footpath and looking over at the house. Elaine may have walked under the house and taken hold of his wooden screwdriver, chisels or paint brushes. She might have put her hand in a pile of wood shavings or spread her hand out on unfinished leather gloves.

I thought of her sitting in his truck, clasping the thin steering wheel and sinking into the leather driver's seat that had formed around George, the arc of his back and the weight of his legs. The windscreen would have been grimy from his cigarette smoke, and his smell still there in the truck.

Maybe she took something away; one of his fibreglass

helmets. There were dozens of them under his bench or in the garden. I used the odd ones, the failures, as plant pots. I filled them with soil and in a strong wind they would rock on the lawn. Maybe she took one of those. A new white one, and put it on her head in the dark.

I did not worry about Elaine so much as her house. I was afraid of finding another George, and myself and our family in the house of a woman I have never met.

I have imagined it many times. A cabinet of dark polished wood with frosted glass at the front and cups, saucers and plates inside. On top of the cabinet, framed pictures of George as a young man with his motorcycle. He is squinting in the sun of some afternoon. A man when I was a girl. Perhaps pictures of him when he was a boy wearing a dark sailor's suit, his hair gleaming with oil. Or as a baby in a white gown. A bit of his past even I have not discovered. And a picture of myself, on a separate ledge, above a room heater or on a bookshelf, with my daughter or nursing my grandchildren.

I stood on the clipped grass in front of the white gate for a moment, the bag of letters at my feet. I thought of leaving it just inside the fence.

But I was attracted by the garden. The front yard was filled with rose bushes. Some of the flowers were huge with interlocking petals and long thorns.

I didn't know how long she had been watching me. I was looking into the biggest white rose I had ever seen. It nodded and scraped the side of a red tin letterbox and flecks of paint had fallen into its centre. I thought I could see paint actually grown into the petals when I looked up and Elaine was there, standing in the doorway.

"Hello Frieda," she said. "Come in."

*

I sat in the bay window in the sunlight that came through the glass and lace curtains. I looked at the curtains and the thousands of holes clotted with dust. Cat hairs were stuck in the lace just above the curved back of the couch, where Elaine's cat walked or sat and gazed outside.

Elaine made tea in the kitchen. I saw her through two doorways, in sections only inches wide beyond the loungeroom door, the twist of a small corridor and into the kitchen. She moved quickly for a woman her age. I could see she was opening a cupboard and only a square patch of her floral dress was visible. Then just an ankle, and leather slip-on shoes. A fake pearl necklace. A wrist watch.

I didn't know what to do with the plastic bag. I put it under my feet but my calves pressed against it. I moved it beside my feet. Finally I pulled it next to me on the couch, and put my arm across it as if it was a child. It was still warm from the sun.

It was not as I expected, the house. There were no wood and glass cabinets or photographs of George and the family. Only stacks of magazines. A solid glass ashtray on a brass stand. An electric fireplace with false logs. A knitting bag and yellow needles poking out the top. Old chairs. An aspidistra on a mantelpiece. Next to the plant was a small white ornament. I was straining to see what it was when Elaine came into the room.

"It's lovely, isn't it?" she said. "I've had it for years." She put down a tray on the side table and lifted the lid of a heavy silver coffee pot. Steam curled over her hand as she stirred the hot tea with a spoon. Her ruby ring fogged over.

"White or black, Frieda?"

"Black, please."

"Sorry about the tea pot. I don't have tea very often."

She gave me a cup and I had a sip. I thought I could taste a coffee essence.

"I knew you would come one day to have tea with me," Elaine said. "What have you brought with you?"

"All your letters to George, and some photographs."

She smiled and brought the tea cup to her mouth. I looked at the coffee pot and saw pink shapes, the reflection of her face, shifting on its rilled surface.

"I was going to burn them," I said, "but I couldn't. I can't burn photographs." I should have left them to the mice, I thought. "He died in his sister's house. It's not far from here."

"I was told that, yes," Elaine said.

"Were you living here then? When he died?"

"Yes," she said. "That's strange isn't it? That he died just over the hill."

I thought of the television antennae and roofs that separated the two houses, the mango trees and fruit bats that flew from one to the other. There was one out the front of our place once, hanging from the electricity wires by its dried claws, rocking in the breeze.

"It was the shell house, wasn't it?" she said.

"Yes. His brother-in-law was a diver."

"The children called it that. The shell house."

For a moment she looked out the bay window and in her glasses I could see a reflection of myself. There were two, one on each lens, with my wavy grey hair lit up by the sunlight and my own glasses somewhere in the darkness of my two faces.

"George always smoked too much," Elaine said. "I think he started me smoking."

I had known from the moment I stepped in the house that she was a heavy smoker. I had lived with that same smell for so long that after a while I didn't notice it, until

118

George died and it gradually disappeared from the house.

She had never married, she told me. She had her cat, and the garden. The rows of roses that surrounded the house and grew best outside the bay window. She emptied her ashtrays there. She had no problems with aphids on the window roses. But they were not pure, and the red roses were streaked with dark lines.

"It reminds me of home, the garden," she said. "I feel safe with the garden."

She spoke of George and the village where she first met him. She went on for ages about the river, the mud, the old slate houses, the fireplaces, the markets. After a while she talked about George as if he still lived there, across the sea.

I passed her the bag of letters and thought she might open it, but I had tied the knots in the string too tightly. She fumbled with the knots and I suggested using a knife or scissors, but she lost interest and left it.

"I have something for you," she said. "You could give it to your grandson or keep it for yourself." She took the small ornament from beside the pot plant and looked at me as she brought it to the couch.

"George made it."

It was one of those plaster statues of a motorcycle and rider. The cycle stood on a chalky base and the rider leaned forward on the white saddle, his head as small and round as a bird's egg. His blank goggles had scratches on the surface, as if made by a pin or tiny steel instrument.

"If you turn it over you can see the thumb print," Elaine said. She turned it in my hands. "Do you see? There. George's thumb."

I couldn't even thank her. I just put it in my handbag. For some reason it made me think of his X-rays. The pictures of his ribs and pelvis that I threw away in grief and wanted back, now that I had his thumb. I wanted the pieces. Maybe a dark hair had lodged somewhere in the plaster motorcycle, a hair that had fallen when the statue was just a tin of plaster and water.

She told me I could catch the bus to Brisbane from the stop across the street. It was getting dark and the streetlights flickered on. I sat alone in the bus shelter and looked at her house.

She had not turned any lights on. I thought I saw her passing windows, but I wasn't sure. It was the day's period of death, as George called it. He never rode at dusk. It was a time of bad light, he said. The moment of dreams when light and dark met. When people in streets or backyards disappeared, and returned. I tried to see through the slats of her backyard fence, when the bus arrived.

I looked again from the bus window and saw the fire. It was only a small fire but I had a clear view from my seat above the fenceline. As the bus driver changed the destination sign to Brisbane, I saw a stooped figure moving around the fire, lifting something with a stick to let the flames eat under it. Funnily enough I didn't see any smoke. At that time of day white smoke would have been almost translucent, I imagined. It must have been black smoke. The smoke of burning plastic.

The China Doves

"I've never told your mother this but I can tell you because you listen. Your grandfather George didn't go to her wedding, you know that. He was a Mason and the Masons in those days, well, they didn't like the Catholics. George was very angry.

"He'd been putting a shilling away each week for your mother so she could have a bit of money when she turned twenty-one. She had her twenty-first birthday not long before her wedding and asked him for the money. He wouldn't give it to her, he was that mean and nasty.

"He bought a new camera with that money. Your mother paid for all the wedding herself. I went to work and saved a bit for her but George didn't pay a penny.

"On the wedding day your mother was a bit uptight. It was hot. She had to ice the wedding cake that morning. George was downstairs the whole time. I don't know what he was doing. He stayed down there. And when your mother went out to pick up the flowers he came upstairs.

"He sat down at the table and, you know how clumsy he was, I've told you before, he put his elbow on a little pile of wrapped tissues and broke the china doves for the

121

top of the cake. Snapped the wings right off with his elbow.

"It was an accident, of course. He didn't know they were there. I'll tell you now, and I've never told this to anyone, George was almost in tears trying to put them back together. I've never seen someone so upset. He tried to glue them back together but it didn't work.

"Anne came back and there was a big fight. I nearly hit her. I told her not to talk to her father like that. It all came out in the open that day. About her marrying a Catholic, everything. He just went back downstairs.

"When she was ready to go to the church she looked beautiful. She really did. The bridesmaids wore silver and purple. I remember when she was a little girl I told her that when she got married I'd like her bridesmaids to wear silver and purple. I saw it in a magazine and liked it. With lilies. I didn't want to know what the bridesmaid's dresses were like just before the wedding, and when I saw them I was so happy. She remembered after all those years, you know. You wouldn't think she would remember, would you?

"Well, George was downstairs and he'd set up his new camera, the one he bought with the money. It was ready, on a tripod, and he'd hung up a sheet, like a real studio, to take a photograph of her in her wedding dress.

"He waited at the bottom of the stairs when the cars arrived and when she came down he asked her if he could take a photograph. She brushed past him and said she was already late and had to go.

"It was terrible. At the church everybody felt sorry for me. For Anne. George not even at the wedding. You can imagine the talk. They came up to me with those faces, like someone has passed away.

"George took our niece to a Girls Brigade display that

122

day, I remember.

"He couldn't do enough for Anne and John after they got married. He bought them a washing machine. I still had to use an old copper.

"He was sorry for what he did, I think. It was like he was trying to make up for it. There wasn't enough time. He died just after you were born. He ran out of time. It was like God was punishing him."

Weddings: The Best Man

The plastic doll was strapped by its feet to the steel emblem of the wedding car. It wore a lace dress the same as the bride, and was showing the raggedness of speed. The Best Man sat in the front seat and watched the undressing of the doll through the windscreen.

Apricot ribbons swooped from the sides of the car to the doll's waist. Its stiff nylon brown hair tore from the forehead. Painted eyebrows arching. The face clipped by the evening insects. The tiny dress, hand-made by the mother of the groom, slipped off a shoulder. The skirt flicked up and the exposed doll faced exhaust from traffic.

"We bought Narelle some sexy underwear," a bridesmaid said. "You should see it."

The other two giggled, their chests heaved. Swirling apricot clouds on dresses. A long thigh. A suspender clip warm from blood.

"Dan should have fun with the nightie. Won't need it tonight but."

The doll was almost bald, its head freckled with holes. The nylon hair fell back, hinged in a clot of glue at the nape of the neck.

As they approached the hotel he thought of the night at the pub, two months ago, when Dan told him Narelle was pregnant. Dan smiled with pride, his thick square glasses absorbing lights, the amber of beer, sequined handbags carried past. They went to the nightclub with the giant neon woman's breast pink and swaying above the front door, and got drunk.

The wedding car drove into the hotel car park. The doll's dress lowered and the hair fell dead. Single strands like whiskers sprouted from the pink scalp. The others walked to the reception room.

The Best Man went to the tattered doll, straightened the dress and tried to put the hair back on the head, but it eased back, as if still facing the wind.

*

"Ladies and gentlemen, will you please welcome, for the first time, Mr and Mrs Daniel Murphy."

The bridal party walked in pairs into the room. It was warm from beery breaths, savouries, concealed sweat. They squinted into a spotlight burning at the top of an aluminium tripod. A thin man stood behind it, taping the event on a video camera.

The cameraman watched the wedding reception, a blue-grained history, on a screen the size of a cigarette packet. Guests wavered in the haze. The tops of children's heads floated across the bottom of the screen and vanished.

Guests applauded until the bride and groom sat at the trestle table draped with white cloth. Flowers scratched the clean surface. Dan held his wife's hand under the table. With his other hand he nervously felt the crusted silver surface of a goblet, borrowed from his father's

125

drink cabinet. The stem was fashioned like an ancient tree, the limbs spread and beaten flat to hold wine. Dan, the darkroom technican, peered over a spray of baby's breath and looked for his family.

*

Dan told him a beautiful girl had started work at the film laboratory. She worked as a print cutter, sitting in the same chair every day and watching thousands of people on paper pass by. She cut each print, often slicing off toes or outstretched hands, scathing a trouser leg or lopping tree branches.

Dan was a developer. He worked in the darkroom all day. He found his way around tanks and tubes with a portable electronic eye that turned everything green.

He fished strips of film from tanks and hung them to dry with bulldog clips. They dangled from the racks like square-edged eels.

The Best Man guessed that when Dan came out of the darkroom the day Narelle arrived he saw her standing in bright light, her brown hair soft, her green eyes swimming, and was instantly attracted. She worked in light and he worked in darkness. Went for her like a crazed moth.

She was from Tasmania. She met an army man and went to Townsville. She was engaged at a young age. One day she came home to their flat and found a one-way flight ticket to Hobart on the kitchen table, between a stainless steel knife and fork. She took a bottle of Scotch from the cupboard and drank it that night. She woke up a day later in a hospital bed, the white sheets folded neatly to her chin. She had damaged her kidney, the doctor told her. Perhaps for life.

Dan was secure. He owned his own portable barbecue

and a tiny yellow sailing boat. He had a good nature. For a girl with a broken engagement and ruined kidney, he must have been a vision coming out of that darkroom, squinting.

They spoke for the first time at a fancy dress party. The theme was Rags to Riches, and Dan wore his father's old maroon suit and yellow paisley tie. He had a felt hat, nibbled by silverfish, pressed down on his head and thongs on his feet. Narelle sat in the corner on a bean bag. She wore a black cocktail dress, false diamond earrings, long black gloves and a head-piece with a giant spiralling feather. He sat on a stool next to her for a while. Foam beads squeaked. They disappeared.

*

The Best Man's parents were on holiday in America. His mother rang on the morning of the wedding, from a pay phone in a bar in Bourbon Street. Drunks wailed under the ocean, through wires. He heard Dixie brass between her delayed phrases.

He thought of America as he sat at the head table, and watched his grandmother. She sat near the centre of the crowded reception room, a shawl around her shoulders. She loved Dan as much as her own grandchildren. A woman with a chipped front tooth sat next to her. He could hear the woman's grating voice over everyone else's. A man in a white jacket sat opposite the woman and told her dirty jokes.

It became noisy, the reception. Dan's brother, a groomsman, drank beer from a jug. Later, he would stand on his head with his mouth open as others threw ice cubes across the room at his red face.

Cigarette smoke began sinking from the ceiling. He

knew his grandmother would have to leave soon because of the smoke. It had given her a life of headaches. His grandfather George was a heavy smoker. Mainly roll-your-own tobacco from yellow satchels. She often had to stand on the back landing when he smoked.

He was told his grandfather hated formal ceremonies. It was an excuse that evolved from his mother's wedding, and became worn and accepted over the years. But it was almost certainly the Catholic thing, his grandmother said. And it was true that he hated dressing up and wearing suits.

The Best Man didn't fully understand the story of his mother's wedding. He just loathed the smell of spilt beer on cloth, the warmth and sourness in a room of too many people. The cheap cut glasses. The tight nylon suit from the hire store.

His grandmother held a tiny crocheted basket. In it was a small slice of cake wrapped in a serviette. The basket had been dipped in sugared water to make it stiff. The cake the same texture in generations of weddings, he thought. The icing always thick enough to preserve the cake for years, so long as it wasn't cut. A monument untouched by ants.

The Best Man thought he heard car engines, but it was a noisy crowd of drinkers leaving the public bar below the reception room. Across the road at the service station a drunk slept next to an illuminated bowser, on a skin of concrete over enormous tanks of fuel.

*

A cat without a tail walked under chairs at Dan's engagement party. Guests sat in the backyard of his parents' home, the chair legs sticking into lawn, and laughed at the funny cat with a stub of a tail. Someone threw melon balls at it.

It was what the Best Man remembered most about the party; the cat, on the outer edge of glow from a string of coloured party bulbs. He drank, and looked for the cat. Later he thought it was watching him through the weed stalks at the back of the yard.

He moved under the green army tent Dan had erected to protect the food and gifts from rain or insects. Narelle stood next to the engagement cake, sucking a cherry from her glass of punch.

"Have you got your big speech ready, Narelle?" he said.

"I ain't giving no speech. I don't have to, do I?"

She held the cherry between molars.

"Of course you do. You have to thank everybody for coming. And for the gifts."

"Rubbish. I'm too nervous. I wish I wasn't here." She giggled with girlfriends and split the cherry with her front teeth.

The cake was shaped like two hearts at odd angles. The pink and blue hearts melded into the colour of fresh bruises. Beside it was a large steel knife with a ribbon tied where the blade met the handle.

"Don't know why we're supposed to have a cake," Narelle said. "Are you supposed to have a cake at an engagement party?"

"Lots of people have engagement cakes," the Best Man said.

"It'll be embarrassing when we have to cut it."

Dan opened gifts. He unwrapped the present from his Best Man and held it in the air. They smiled at each other. It was a small ornament, a dark, metal pelican sitting on a piece of dry wood. Below the wood a changing sea for the pelican, a warm television set, a glass coffee table, pile carpet. The pelican's webbed feet were tacked to the wood.

The bar was an old table under the clothesline. Someone had not speared the keg properly and foam gushed from the tap. Buckets of it were thrown over the back fence onto a neighbour's vegetable patch.

The Best Man watched the waves of foam and thought of the cat walking between the damp carrot heads and pumpkins, slowly lifting its paws, trying to work out the smell of malt and soil. He wondered what happened to the cat and where its missing tail was.

Dan and Narelle cut the cake three times. The relatives wanted photographs of the event. The cuts were parallel, hiding the previous cut with the thick blade of the knife. Everybody at the party knew the cake had three cuts, but the photographs would show only one.

The Best Man was one of the last to leave the engagement party. Chairs rested upside down in shadows. The grass was bruised and flattened from shoe heels. Only crumbs remained on the foil base of the engagement cake. He looked for the cat with no tail, but it had gone, disappeared beyond the weeds. He urinated on the wheel of a gravel truck parked in the street, and drove home.

*

The men's suits were oddly shaped. Saggy and buckled from the bodies of other men before them. Air-filled pockets above the knees. Stretched waistlines. Elbow bone grooves in jacket sleeves. Stains had been removed by cleaners. The Best Man found tobacco crumbs in his jacket pocket. He flicked them onto the floor.

Hours before, the suits had rested in clear plastic bags

on Dan's bed and the groom's official party had their names scratched in ballpoint pen on pink tags attached to the hangers. Dan's relatives ate cold ham sandwiches and salad in the kitchen of his mother's house before the wedding. They drank beer and wine. They smelled of soap and did not know where to stand or sit in the chaos of a family before a ceremony.

There were arguments. Brothers and sisters shouted over the whine of a hair dryer in the bathroom. Toothpaste dropped from a brush and landed on freshly polished shoes. It was humid and steam lingered after repeated showers.

The groom and his party sat downstairs and had a quiet drink. The walls of Dan's room were covered with pennants, car posters, a clock in the centre of a fake tennis racquet, and a crucifix that glowed in the dark. They almost whispered. Chuckled at the din from upstairs. Thought of the bride and her bridesmaids in a room in a distant suburb. Soon they would all join at a single point. For a moment, in the pale green light from a window of leafy vines, they felt like men together.

They changed into their suits in the small room. Elbows knocked as they took out the white shirts. They felt uncomfortable in the strange suits, still warm from the plastic bags that had been in the back of a car. They buffed their shoes. All of them had difficulty fastening the bow tie clips and standing back to back in a circle they fastened each other's, checking the tightness around the neck then turning and correcting the straightness. Just before they left, Dan's mother came downstairs and pinned pink carnations on their lapels. The flowers were still moist from the refrigerator.

They drove to the church in Dan's cream sedan. He was nervous behind the wheel. The Best Man looked at him, and thought of his friend only hours before in football shorts and a striped T-shirt.

Now his hair was immaculate. Stiff, ginger hair parted down the middle, against his usual grain of brushing, and swept back by a hair dryer. It was motionless in a net of hair spray.

"Do you like it? Mum did it," Dan said.

*

The Best Man tried to imagine his parents' wedding. He had seen photographs of his mother, a cooking demonstrator, leaning over a cake with an icing tube in her hands on the morning of her wedding. Her skin the colour of the ivory-handled knife next to the cake. His father on the church steps, a young bank teller wearing a perfect suit.

His parents had honeymooned on the Hawkesbury River in a varnished cabin cruiser. Long days of fishing and glare. At night, looking at the stars above the tall trees on the river bank and talking about their future. Children. About him.

He wished they were at Dan's wedding. His mother had asked him to make up a telegram to read at the reception. From America, his mother dictated the ideas on the telephone. She spoke in short, telegram sentences. He took the fake telegram from his pocket and read it after the speeches. Everyone thought it had come all the way from America. It briefly took the wedding beyond the hotel reception room, the hinterland township of Nerang. Dan and Narelle were stunned. America.

The Best Man took the piece of paper from the pile of telegrams and put it in his trouser pocket. It would not be treasured in a shoe box years later.

At the end of the reception the guests gathered in a circle on the dance floor. As the farewell music played the circle stretched into an egg shape. The bride and groom moved in opposite directions, to each guest. The chain of people swayed, broke, rejoined. Faces were kissed. Hands clasped. The old aunts cried.

The newlyweds led the guests into the car park. Dan's car looked a part of the ragged hotel landscape. Newspapers were tangled around tyres. Branches poked from the passenger windows. Streamers webbed the vehicle to the asphalt. They could smell lemon shaving cream. Cans on string were tied to the bumper bar, hidden in shadow.

The Best Man patted Dan on the shoulder as he stepped into the car. There was too much colour and disorder to talk. A tiny circus. Sentiments had been discarded in the vanished egg of guests. The night had become charged with a peculiar energy, a moment of scission like lightning searing air. People were yelling and hooting and nothing made sense. The Best Man held his girlfriend around the waist and stood with the others. Confetti was carried onto the road by a gust of wind.

Sitting in the front seat, her dress streaked with oil from the car door hinges, Narelle could have been anyone. The Best Man's sister. Girlfriend. Even his mother. He felt for an instant that time was no longer fixed but shimmering, like the crowns of trees.

Dan waved as he cruised out of the car park. Screaming men swinging coats above their heads ran after the car until they couldn't keep up. Two small red lights and a golden spray of sparks. Even when the car was beyond sight they could hear the tinkling cans, for minutes, down the highway.

Bias

I can see the bowling club from the verandah. I sit on an old vinyl chair beneath the watery hands of poinciana leaves that form a canopy over the back of my house. The house has a new tin roof and already is covered in possum claw scratches. Even the branches that hang over the verandah have orange wounds. It is a nice tree, but it is not mine. The roots and trunk are in the neighbour's yard, and the branches are over the fence. I sit and watch the bowlers.

They glide at this distance. The slow bend of the legs. Curved spines and stretched cotton. That graceful semi-circular movement of their arms. I cannot see the black bowl after it is released from the fanned hand, but it rolls behind the ridge of earth and grass. In the early afternoon I see the occasional glint from spectacles, or an unfinished glass of squash and ice on the clubhouse verandah.

A loudspeaker is attached to the guttering at the corner of the clubhouse. The bowlers have days when only women and only men play, and on the ladies' days tangled names and numbers are pushed through the speaker and a voice comes across the oval next to the club, to my

134

verandah. The voice is thin when it reaches me, having travelled over wooden benches, grass, rubbish bins, trees, parked cars.

Once, I thought I heard them call my mother's name through microphone and wire. But my mother has never played bowls. She lives down the coast, in the hinterland, away from the bowling clubs near the beaches. After all, it is an old person's game, my mother says.

My father plays bowls in front of their house, where I sometimes stay for weekends. He loves playing all games and has a camphorwood chest full of them in his billiard room. Mah-jong tiles he has never touched. A chess game with the pieces all Hollywood characters: Marilyn Monroe the Queen, W.C. Fields the King, the pawns Keystone Kops with tiny batons.

He bought a leather sack of imported Italian bowls and tried to get my mother to play, on the front lawn. He told me proudly the bowls were made of compressed wood. He bounces them on the springy grass. The bowls rarely go straight for him and the grass takes hold of them short of the jack. A stronger swing and they go sailing down the hill. It is really the spirit of the game, without precision, when my father plays.

I thought I heard my mother's name again one afternoon, and walked down to the oval. It was almost dusk and they were still playing. I sat on a bench when the runners came. They run between the oiled lines of the oval. It is hard to see the lines at that time of day. You can hear the runners before you see them, their scissoring arms and legs at sharper angles than that of the bowlers. Heaving chests. Sweat onto grass. They appear from nowhere, run a few laps and spiral off into a sidestreet. I hear the flap of their laces as they disappear in the dark.

The bowlers have gone but the runners keep coming. Even late at night some of them circle the oval, stepping onto the oil strips, guided only by headlights from passing traffic. The old runners, slightly faster than a walk, on the inside lane. And the young runners striding past, lapping them. A constant shift of being behind, flowing through and being ahead again.

*

My parents wanted two things when I went on my holiday to Europe. My father wanted a small indoor bowls set from England. The type you play in corridors, on smooth carpet. My mother wanted a photograph of the London church where her father George sang in the choir as a boy. I found the church before I left, in a tourist guide. It was on a map. A child-like ink sketch of it, with a spire and cross, in a grid of streets.

*

My journey was a red line, a vein that, at first, swooped over ranges and salt pans, over jungle, sand, then over the page of the airlines map I found in the front pocket of a seat. I nearly lost my route amongst other lines that stemmed from the cities. The lines hopped from one red dot to another and tied up the whole world as if it was a parcel. I could trace my destination backwards and forwards. I calculated distances at the start then gave up. After a day in the plane I arrived at another airport terminal.

I had to pass through long, windowless corridors that

opened into circular waiting rooms of glass and blue plastic chairs, then continued on the other side. My luggage came out on a conveyor belt at the intersection of five corridors. Men in uniforms and caps glided past on children's bicycles.

Outside, trucks and cars were covered in snow. I saw giant cranes beyond the airport fence. The red line had ended. I moved onto black lines then. The fractures of a new map. The trains.

*

I heard of the shell in my childhood. George's sister, Nell, had gone to London after his death. Not straight after he died, in her house in the loungeroom chair, but later. She took her favourite shell, as big as a man's open palm, its edges almost opaque. In the light, pink and blue waves stretched across its surface. The beginnings of a pearl, an oblong swell, had formed near its base.

She carried the shell halfway across the world, in a straw bag, to the church. She gave it to the pastor in memory of George who had sung there, a schoolboy in shorts that covered his knees, a striped tie, a cap. George, the choir boy. His young voice lost now to the rafters. Perhaps the notes lodged in wooden beams, like hooks. In the pores of the stone columns. Nell said the pastor could use the shell for baptisms, to scoop water out of the font. It was the last story we heard of the shell. I was to see if it was still there. To see if George had become part of the church's history.

I fed pigeons in the square with grain from a plastic cup. I took photographs of them, their feet blurred and heads striking seed a smudged curve in the pictures. I took a photograph of a girl sitting on the head of a giant

137

metal lion, gripping the surface of its mane.

The church was on the edge of the square. Inside, men slept on benches, their feet on the armrests. Others sat and stared at their feet. It was warm in the church. At the back, looking down to the altar, I could smell damp hair and cigarette smoke, socks and varnished wood. Walking down the aisle there was a point where the human smell gave way to the scent of flowers, and further just the freshness of roses and lilies in brass pots. Through cloth book marks, candles.

I asked the flower lady at the front about the shell. I told her of the boy, George, and the journey of the shell in the straw bag. I couldn't see a baptism font.

She asked me to wait and went through a doorway beside the altar into a room. It was filled with ivory light, from a high window, and hymn books were stacked on the floor. The spines curling, worn through by decades of hands. A banister and a small stairwell went down under the church. A young pastor and the woman appeared from its well. She explained to him, before me, about the shell.

"I was wondering if it was still here," I said. "It was a long time ago, I know."

"A shell," he said. "A small shell?"

"I don't know," I said. "I've never seen it."

He went back into the room. A man started snoring and muttered something in his sleep. A few words, a tiny echo that dissolved in archways.

"Would this be what you're looking for?" the pastor said when he returned. In his hands was a shell with an ornate silver handle attached to its base. An engraver's tool had removed the young pearl.

I took it and ran my fingers along its worn edge, brushed my thumb across its surface. It was not a relic, a treasure to me. I had only heard of it. Holding the cold handle I thought it was fairly unremarkable. I liked the shell of the stories better.

"It has been used for every baptism here for more than twenty years," the pastor said.

That was all he knew of the shell. Was the man George a pearl diver in Australia, he asked. Had there been a pearl in the shell?

I asked the flower lady to take a photograph of me with the shell, for my mother, to prove that it still existed. I had no flash for my camera and stood beneath the stained glass window, behind the altar, where there was the most light.

I held the shell in front of me and thought, as I smiled at the flower lady, that my mother might never see the shell. Just the photograph. It was a shadowy picture, I discovered later, despite the coloured light from the window. The flowers dark shapes. Blackness around the edges. I am not smiling because the flower lady was so slow in taking the shot, her thick glasses pressed against the viewfinder, her finger searching for the button. You can just see the shell. Like a small grey fish, sleeping in my hands.

*

My grandmother gave me a list of places to look for when I was in England, written on a sheet of letter paper and folded in an envelope. Her writing was crooked, although there were pale blue lines on the paper.

On some lines she had just written words. Reading. Scarborough. Under other names she wrote phrases. "Went there for summer when I was a kid, before I came out to Brisbane. Pebbles on the beach. Pier. Birds up on the bluff. Gladys nearly drowned there." "Steel fence and small garden patch out the front. Grandad sits there in the sun in the mornings and tips his hat to everyone." She wrote as if her world of memory was still there. The same shadows against red brick. Her father on the wooden stool with the newspaper. Dust in his old boot laces.

I hired a car. It was easy to get out of London and onto the motorways with their several lanes. Further, flat fields that stretched for miles, farm houses, cottages, cow specks, tractors tearing the earth.

I stayed the first night at a name off my grandmother's list. A small town by the sea with rows of houses nestled not far from a cliff. I stayed in a Bed and Breakfast only metres from the cliff edge and in the morning could see, from my bed, just the sea and sky in the window.

At the base of the cliff was a small beach. A cream bathing pavilion and fun parlours had been built into massive rock cuts. The fun parlours were closed, with thick salt and spray on their front windows. At the end of the short row of buildings was an old merry-go-round, the horses wrapped in plastic for the winter months. I could see their eyes through the clear plastic. Thick black eyelashes and solid ears. Gold and black tails.

I took my grandmother's list out of my leather jacket and halfway down, beneath the name of the town by the sea, was written "Went there when I was five. Horses dancing on the beach."

*

I had trouble with the roundabouts. I spread out a map on the passenger seat of the car. I had the entire country there, inside green borders. The cities were aflame, a fusing of red highways and yellow squares. There were so many names on the map some overlapped others. Some names were bent in the middle and others, along the coast, extended over the sea like jetties.

The map was too small to show the roundabouts. The first one I struck was so big I didn't realise I was on it. I was heading north and by the time I saw the sign I had passed the turnoff, caught in the inside lane by trucks, cars. I went around again and darted out of the circle of road. I got caught on many more.

Later, I asked a woman at a hotel desk if there were any maps that showed roundabouts. When they would appear. How far apart they were spaced so I could be prepared. The woman said no such maps existed.

*

My week became a succession of castles. My favourite was the castle of wax figures. In each room there were lifesize men and women, in black suits and lace gowns. A woman stood beside a piano, a soaring falsetto voice coming from behind an aspidistra on a stand. A man sat at the piano, his fingertips poised above the keys.

In the next room two men sat smoking. One sucked on a pipe. The other was lighting a cigarette and held a match in a cupped hand. An intermittent glow from his palm lit up his face. I tried to look into the scalloped gaps between his fingers but from behind a red rope, standing on a plastic strip for tourist feet, I could not see the source of light or the wires connected to the tiny bulb in his hand. I thought about the cigarette smoker as I walked into the next room. The wire would have to be in his arm. A warm vein in wax, perhaps connected to a battery lodged in the base of his spine, if he had one.

I saw a beautiful woman in the next room. A maid. She emptied a pitcher of water into a man's bath, her body slightly bent at the waist. He stood behind her, in a robe, looking out the window at the peacocks on the lawn. I could only see her profile. A strand of hair fell across her forehead. She seemed to be smiling, but it may have been the strain of holding the pitcher that pulled upward that side of her wax lips.

Maybe there was nothing on the other side of her face. It may have been blank. She may have had one eye, a sunken cheek. She was still beautiful and I remembered her for a long time after, in that room filled with the pale green music of running water.

*

I had always wanted to see Stonehenge. I remembered the black and white photographs in my school history book, the sun through its side. Diagrams from above. Dots that showed the circles, the trenches, the stones that had fallen and been propped up by men down the centuries.

The signs to Stonehenge were clearly marked. From miles away over grassy fields I could see it. Closer, through the drizzle, were dozens of buses in the car park next to it. They were the same height as the monument and people moved between them.

I parked amongst the buses and walked, with others, through the tunnel that passed under the road and up the ramp to the stones. Glass booths stood crookedly on the grass. Guard boxes with gold handles and red cushions, and books and cups inside. A new bitumen path circled the stones. Ropes sagged from post to post.

142

People read history from black placards.

I studied the stones for marks, cuts, scars from rope, ancient symbols of eyes or fire, the sun or time, but there was just dull rock. Lichen. Some hairline fractures. Others peered into the circle, looking for axe heads or animal-skin boots, I imagined. Just some sign of men and women, long dead. Instead they could see people on the other side of the circle holding colourful umbrellas. Silent, looking at each other through gaps in the configuration.

I followed the path around to the other side. It ended close to a fence that ran alongside the road. A bulb of raw earth, worn inches into the ground, was at the end of the path. It was there, I presumed, that people stood to take photographs when the sun lowered to the level of the stones. Tourists from around the world, on that bare patch.

I bought a booklet before I left. The history of Stonehenge. Fragments of animal skin, bone, deer antlers had been found at the base of the stones, it said. Packing, to hold them up.

I drove away. A black cake in the rear vision mirror. A gathering of ants.

*

I went to the village where my grandfather was born. My grandmother describes it on her list as quaint, with tiny streets, a river and ducks. I thought I could find the street where he lived, running off a main road.

The village had become a major resting point for drivers, between two cities. A knot of expressways, exit and entrance ramps. It was Saturday when I arrived. I stopped at a motorway restaurant and asked a woman for directions. She took my grandmother's list and checked the address.

I found the street but didn't have a house number. There were rows of townhouses, gardens, bicycles, doorknobs, milk bottles, brick steps. I stood in the middle of the street and took a photograph of one end, towards the shopping centre, and the other end, cut short by a railway line. Later, when I showed my grandmother the pictures, she thought she could see the right house, but wasn't sure.

She said the different colours of the houses confused her. Green window ledges, yellow doors, foot-high numbers and small brass ones on letterboxes. I thought of men and women, after a night at the pub perhaps, going through the wrong gate and trying to open doors with keys that would never fit.

*

I flew home at the start of spring on the same red arcs of the airline map.

*

They said I looked older when I got home. That I had broader shoulders. Veins that stood out in my arms. My mother stood me against my father, back to back, and even said I had grown taller.

*

I don't think it will be long before my father takes up

proper amateur lawn bowls. He shook my hand when I gave him the English indoor bowls set, and swept the corridor and billiard room floor.

My mother says that late at night, when he cannot sleep, he plays bowls in the room downstairs, beneath their bedroom, and that the clack of wood keeps her awake for hours.

Blue Overalls

The birds waited for the red tractor, behind bowls of plastic flowers and rose bushes. When it came they skipped across sheets of marble. Fluttered from cross ledges. Brown birds, hazy with lice, through the fresh grass clippings. The noise of the tractor did not scare the birds. He could see them, close to the blades the tractor towed, as he drove past the cemetery. On the hill, weaving through stone, the machine kicked waves of grass and seeds into the air.

His grandmother lived near the cemetery. He was surprised that she had telephoned so early. He said he would visit before he went to see his parents on the Gold Coast for the weekend.

He drove his green Ford down winding streets, into the gully of poincianas. Leaves rotted on front lawns. Others were crushed on the road, or picked up by moist car wheels and carried to suburbs where there were no poincianas.

It had changed over the years, his grandmother's street. It had become an area of students and dogs. The late night twang of guitar. Beer and wine bottles in gutters on Sunday mornings. It was not unusual for dogs to

walk into living rooms on summer evenings. A bull terrier called Prickle had fallen asleep under a tree in his
grandmother's front yard, and never woken.

He remembered Beck Street as a child, travelling on
the vinyl upholstery of his mother's station wagon. Ice
block sticks coated with sand on the car floor. Celery
heads whispering in grocery bags.

He drove past the same unpainted wooden house on
the corner, with the weeds around its stumps. Purple-
headed flowers. Once, he had looked into the open
bedroom window of the house and saw a young woman,
in the gloom, wearing a white bra and looking at herself
in a mirror. He glanced again into the window, still
open, but saw nothing.

The street was dotted with black bitumen patches
which had sunk or broken up at the edges. For decades
workmen had laboured at joining new and old bitumen.

His grandmother's house could no longer be seen
from the top of the street. It was in the shadow of a
brick block of flats which were so close his grandmother
said she could hear bobby pins dropped in bathtubs. It
was nothing to hear several people stirring their coffee in
the mornings, she said. Curtains wafted out above her
rusted guttering.

An old woman called Alice had lived in a house on the
land where the flats were built. He remembered her, sitting in the darkness on a couch. She wore thin floral
dresses, cardigans and always had her silver hair in a
bun. Once, when he went inside the old colonial with his
grandmother, a mouse skipped across the hallway from
one room to another. It ran so fast its feet barely touched linoleum roses. The house smelt of nests, sour milk
and the old woman.

The flats were built shortly after Alice died. She was
born in the house and lived there for over a hundred

years and when she died her grandsons had the house flattened in a month. The yellow machines moved in and gouged the earth, upturning creek silt and old bottles. When the flats went up it became cold in his grandmother's house. Slivers of sun bounced off some unit windows and onto her fibro house. The television went out of focus. Newsreaders appeared, their ghosts in suits beside them.

He walked up the back stairs of the house because she was usually in the kitchen. She ironed clothes there, wrote letters, drank tea and battled against ants.

"Gran? Hello?"

"Hello love. I'm in the bathroom."

She was scrubbing a mirror. She was standing on a chair and the hem of her dress swayed as she squeaked the cloth against her own reflection.

"You want me to put the kettle on?" he said.

She came into the kitchen, her hair held back by bobby pins.

"Phew. I've been cleaning all day."

"Sit down for a while," he said, firing the flint gun at the gas ring. It exploded and warmed the skin of his hand, singeing hair.

"Is it hot?" she said, dabbing her forehead with a handkerchief. A mower buzzed in someone's yard, beyond fences and washing lines held up by old-fashioned wooden props.

"John comes this afternoon," she said.

John the gardener came every second Friday. He was a pensioner, filling in time, earning some extra money. He wore a cream canvas cap with tiny mesh air holes in the sides. The old man struggled with the mower, along the outer edge of the yard and then inwards, circling the giant poinciana tree that grew in the middle.

The tree's roots were so big they surfaced across the

yard. Knuckles rose through the grass. The mower blades struck them and bit into the wood. The roots had even shattered the concrete surrounding the flats. Another section of pathway was beginning to lift, but nobody seemed to notice.

John mowed over the poinciana pods which exploded in stringy shards. He dumped the grass clippings in the incinerator in the corner of the yard, drank a glass of lime cordial with ice cubes that was always offered to him, took his money and left. He avoided awkward patches of weeds and skirted fallen pegs or cat bowls.

"I'll do it for nothing you know, Gran."

"You're too busy. You don't want to be working around your old Granny's yard all the time."

She said the same thing every time he offered.

The phone rang. It was her sister, Gladys. They rang each other once, sometimes twice a day. They talked about small things. A new sponge for the kitchen sink. A dog that had scared the cat. An old lady in the next street who had died from the sting of a bee.

He went into the loungeroom and sat in a chair next to a marble and steel coffee table. He remembered the furniture from home, years ago. A wide crack stretched across the table's surface. His grandmother had placed a lace doily over it. A vase of flowers, hand-picked from the tree at the bottom of the front stairs, stood on the table. Some of the flowers were turning brown.

Next to the vase was a framed picture of his sister in her wedding gown. People stood in groups, behind her shoulders. He was there somewhere in a black tuxedo. A pink rose on his lapel. Relatives had asked him when he, the twin brother, would marry. He smiled, and drank. Lost the flower during the night. His girlfriend had it in her handbag the next day.

He took the photograph albums from under the coffee table. He knew the albums well. Recognised the faces of strangers and relatives he knew nothing about. Others, captured standing with their hands in their pockets, or talking, their mouths open. The paper his grandfather used to print the pictures on was thin and blue. He had developed the films in the darkroom sink, downstairs.

There is a picture of George sitting on a post by the sea. Rocks and shale at his feet. His left leg bent. His right straight. Boots murky and scuffed in the blue. Baggy pants. He wears a blazer made for a bigger man, with a handkerchief poking from his top pocket. A wide-brimmed hat on his head. A shadow arcing across his forehead. Three small waves curl, at the point of breaking, behind him.

"I found her lying in the wheelbarrow downstairs," his grandmother said into the phone. "It was full of old leaves and rubbish and I told her she'd get pneumonia and should come upstairs and we had a cup of tea, poor thing."

A picture of an old truck with wood-spoked wheels. Glistening rubber tyres. The spare balanced on the running board. Blurred tin sheds in the background. A fresh sign on the side of the truck. Cribb Island Bakery. Spidery twirls painted in the corners of the sign. The smell of bread from the back of the truck, through wooden side panels. Thousands of crumbs in cracks, inching into the truck's workings.

"Take two of those and it will go away," she told Gladys. "I'll have to go up and see the doctor again soon too. Up on Wickham Terrace."

A blue photograph taken under the house. His grand-
'ther dressed and ready for war. Sitting on a beam bet-
¬ two stumps. His legs apart. He holds a slouch hat
¬n his legs and looks away. For a battle, or embar-

rassed that he'll never see action. Behind him the darkness under the house, fusing with the edges of the picture.

"And don't be afraid of the rain. They said on the news it was only light showers. No lightning. I'll call you tomorrow."

His favourite photograph of his grandfather was the one that was so dark he could hardly find the figures in it. George in overalls. The sleeves rolled up to the elbows. He stands next to a street gutter. White stars, his thumbnail and watch. His right hand on his hip. A worker's beret worn at an angle. The mouth a serious line of blue. Behind him, leaning against a wooden fence, is a young woman. She wears a frilly dress and a hat shaped like a bell. She looks at George. He looks strong, in the overalls, a cigarette smouldering in his left hand. The grandfather he never met, but thought he knew, flat on a piece of paper he could have fitted in his top pocket.

"You're not looking at those photographs again," his grandmother said.

"I like looking at them."

"You've seen them dozens of times."

"I never get sick of them," he said.

She moved past him and stood on the front landing. She could see the old bakery on the hill in Stevenson Street. George had once painted a sign on its wall. Now there was a new sign advertising a restaurant. It was painted in a 1930s style with pictures of American hoodlums, cigars, dancing girls and strings of beads. George's sign was there somewhere, beneath the scars of a gangster's face.

"You know they've turned the bakery into a fancy restaurant," she said.

"Some of my friends have been there. Reckon it's

151

pretty good. Anywhere with booze is good to them."

"For the young people," she said. "I thought so. Your mother used to go up there when she was little and buy a loaf of bread. She'd eaten the middle out of the whole loaf by the time she got home. How's Rachael anyway? I haven't seen her for ages."

"Neither have I," he said.

"You're not going out with her any more?"

"We broke up ages ago."

"She was a lovely girl too. I suppose you've met someone new already."

"Maybe," he said.

"I don't want to hear about it," she said, laughing.

He closed the albums and put them at his feet. There were more photographs in a suitcase under the bed in the spare room. A cream suitcase heavy with prints of relatives, friends, dogs, shop owners, riders, women, cats, cars, trees, helmets, gloves and children, all pressed tightly against each other.

"I'll sort through those other photographs for you one day, Gran," he said.

"Just stay there," she said. "I have something for you."

He heard the creak of her wardrobe door. All her treasures were there, in mothball fumes. She returned with a small leather case, its sides scratched like the hide of cattle.

"I've been keeping this for you for a long time," she said. "It's about all I have left of your grandfather."

She had difficulty opening the suitcase. The two rusted latches eventually flicked open. She took out some old papers, cards, photographs, and a plastic bag. The plastic was soft and crazed with creases.

"George used to draw, you know that," she said. "He held onto a few things his whole life. He was silly that way. He'd keep a shirt until it fell apart. Or a belt. And he kept a notebook."

She took the book out of the bag. It had been damaged by insects and mould. It was also stained with oil, and the pages were loose.

"Like a diary sort of thing," his grandmother said. "It's got some drawings in it. Just some doodles and sketches he did when he was younger."

He opened the notebook and felt the spine shift against his fingers. He knew something like this existed. Something that could take him beyond the photographs, into them, and bring him a little closer to understanding his grandfather.

"You might think this is a bit funny but I kept his old overalls," she said. "He used to wear them all the time."

He looked at her face as she handed him the overalls in the plastic bag. Her eyes were moist. Her skin soft. Wrinkles like the accidental flicks of a pencil.

"He should have met you," she said. She stood up. "I'm making more tea. Do you want some?"

He stayed in the loungeroom, the notebook and overalls in his hands. A light rain began to fall and looking outside he felt he had been let in on an old secret, that the glass lid of a museum cabinet had been lifted and he had been allowed to touch precious objects, breath in the stale air of decades. The warm scent of soil rose up against the rain.

*

The expressway weaved above the banks of the Brisbane River. Huge white pylons sat in mud, brushed by mangroves. He wondered if there were derelicts under the bridges and expressways as he drove. Building fires on mud beneath slabs of concrete and steel.

It was difficult to escape the new expressway to the coast. Cars surged forward between white guard rails and fencing. The exit ramps were clearly marked, the names of main roads and the distances to them in metre-high letters and figures. He flowed with the traffic, boxed in by other cars. Restricted by the gunshot bubbles that separated lanes.

The overalls and notebook were against his left thigh on the bench seat. At times he could see the old coast road, a band of bitumen, that ran parallel to the expressway. It would disappear on a curve, vanish beneath the car park of a suburban tavern, then emerge beside a paddock or petrol station.

His parents had spoken of the old road. Of rounded black cars with big silver fenders parked next to creeks or pie stands. Of families sharing a thermos of tea and sandwiches halfway to Southport.

It was an outing, a weekend adventure to go to the coast in those days. A pleasant drive, especially through Beenleigh, where the cows grazed close to the road, behind a wire fence. Cows used to the hum of traffic, the flashing car steel in their moon eyes. Bushland so close to the road the gums dropped seeds on the bitumen and when they were crushed by rubber wheels they smelled of oil and ants.

The expressway was raised slightly above the level of the paddocks. Above backyards with their rows of barbecues and incinerators. The new bitumen was already streaked with tyre marks. Screech lines that swayed from lane to lane or into solid walls of granite. His mind drifted in the boredom of the expressway. Passing trucks always brought him back to the road, with their tangle of radio wires and floral curtains. Or the hiss of sports cars.

He wanted to stop and read the notebook, feel the soft overalls again. But he couldn't stop. He was pushed on by other cars, and the dropping petrol gauge in his old Ford.

He enjoyed being alone in the car, playing his favourite music on a tape machine and smoking cigarettes. Sometimes he sang at the top of his voice as he drove past the new housing estates with their thin trees all the same distance apart, and the bulldozers bunched in the middle of the partly cleared earth. Past the box church and statue of an Australian soldier leaning on a stone rifle, the shadow of the soldier's slouch hat creeping onto the northbound highway in the afternoon.

And just when he thought he could drive on forever he arrived at the Farm Fresh Eggs sign and the first set of traffic lights since the city. From there it was just a quick turn off the highway, through the tunnel of gums, lawns and letterboxes, and into the driveway of his parents' home.

*

His parents set up a bedroom for him in the white brick garage that faced the valley. It was separate from the house, down a twist of mud and straw stairs, beside his father's vegetable garden and banana trees. They figured that since he had been living away from home, although he was only an hour's drive away, he was a man and needed independence.

He had a bed in the corner of the garage, near the pipes and timber framing of an unfinished bathroom cubicle, a circular mat on the concrete, a fold-up card table for a desk, and bookshelves.

In the afternoons he would slide open the roller doors

and sit and read in the sun, beside the family's orange speed boat. The tin roof creaked. Mice journeyed through bags of old clothes, nibbled on blocks of foam and paper. The banana trees hissed near the back windows, and at night he could hear the chuckles and fighting of bats tearing into the fruit.

Often he had watched his father through the windows, digging in the small vegetable patch, stooped over radishes and lettuce. His father struggled with the two acres of land. On weekends he wore his radio headphones with their tiny aerial, strapped the weed clipper over his shoulders and plodded through the undergrowth like a man searching for mines. By the time he cleared one area another had started to thicken, ragged and lush in corners of the yard. The land was too much for one man to handle, his father said.

His parents were not home when he arrived that afternoon. He went into the garage and threw his bag on the bed, opened the roller doors and sat in his chair with the overalls and notebook on his lap.

The sun illuminated piles of family rubbish in the garage. Old exercise books. His father's college yearbooks and a bag of rowing pennants with red poinsettia leaves and crossed oars stitched onto white felt. A large buckled poster of his mother, a beach beauty queen in the summer of 1959, held up by the arms of lifesavers, their curved caps at the base of the picture. A bag of marbles. A clay teapot. Wood.

He opened the yellow pages of the notebook. Not every page had been used. There were drawings, blobs of ink over phrases, pencil sketches. Pictures of animals wearing army uniforms, hats and boots. Carrying rifles. A paragraph of tight handwriting near the book's string hinge.

"They tell me I cannot go to war because I have flat

156

feet. Start work next week at the hangar painting
aeroplanes. They want me to paint a bloody tennis court
on the top of a fuel storage tank."

There were drawings of fantasy. A horseman holding
a flag, the black horse standing on its hind legs, its
muscles just curves of ink. A pencil drawing of an old
roadster, its headlights like eyes and the fender bending
into a grin. In the car, a man with a flowing scarf and a
woman wearing a beret.

The poems were written in neat squares in the centre
of pages. Finely printed, the ink pale.

At The Tea Table

This fragile cup will break at last
In spite of my endeavour,
But friendship's bonds which hold us fast,
They endure forever.

Our world will pass, our little day
We dreamed would leave us never,
But all the loving things we say,
These will last forever.

He looked into the valley for a moment and tried to
imagine George, sitting in the kitchen of the fibro
house, writing the words. A grown man with a reputa-
tion for speed and swearing, cigarettes and the company
of men, trying to distil a moment at the kitchen table in
some forgotten evening in Brisbane.

The children's poems were dated years before the
birth of George's only child. Before his marriage to
Frieda. The verse nestled in sketches of boys and girls at
play. Or in old bathtubs held above floorboards by the
feet of lions.

Conkers

I never could resist to pick
A conker from the roads,
And often I've come trotting home
With most enormous loads.

One day I'll build a house of clay
And while the walls are soft,
I'll press in conkers all around
And hoist a flag aloft.

He flicked through dozens of blank pages, straining
at the cotton binding, and found a passage that looked
like it had been written quickly, at an angle.

Oh Ages fade and centuries die,
Time garners them all silently,
But fresh and sweet is the morning air.

The sun disappeared behind the hills. It would be light
for another half an hour, and it was quiet except for the
hum of the freezer at the back of the garage. A freezer
full of coral trout from his father's last fishing trip up
north.

He stood up, put the notebook on the warm seat and
took the overalls out of the plastic bag. He held them
up. Worn and soft cloth. The buttons still tightly sewn
on.

Quickly, he slipped the overalls over his clothes. They
were baggy and a bit short in the legs, but the old
material was comfortable. He looked down at himself.
He could have been any mechanic or house painter.
Overalls had not changed through the years, he thought,

except for the invention of zips. He walked around on the grass in front of the garage. Watched the cloth billow around his legs as it would have done when his grandfather walked. As it did with any man.

He took them off and pushed them into the bag. He would not wear them again. They would remain in the bag and be viewed through clear plastic. He put the notebook on his bookshelf.

His parents were still not home. It was almost dark. He took hold of the weed clipper and checked the fuel tank. It was almost full and he pumped the red fuel button and put his arms through the harness. He started the small motor and oily blue smoke belched into the garage.

He began in the corner of the yard behind his bedroom window. The tall weeds swayed, swollen with fluid. He clutched the hand accelerator and slashed at their base. A mesh of strands and flying seeds. He cut small paths into the patch, and thrilled at the motor's vibration through his hands. The power to clear tangled growth he could not have walked through moments before.

It was night and he continued to cut. Falling stalks brushed against his bare legs. Seeds caught on the hairs of his arms. He would cut until the fuel ran out.

On the verandah of a neighbour's house, in the glow of an amber light, a man and his wife looked towards the garage in search of the night weed cutter and his whining motor, and saw a pair of white shorts, as dull as a distant star, in the darkness.